Moving Melody

By E Dee Merriken Monnen

E Dee Merriken Monnen

ISBN: 978-1-969021-58-9 (ebook)
ISBN: 978-1-969021-56-5 (Paperback)
ISBN: 978-1-969021-57-2 (Hardcover)

Using humor, romance, and drama Moving Melody tells the story of Melody Vanders, a woman in her early twenties, who witnesses a research scientist being kidnapped in a busy airport by known assassins. After the scientist is found dead in a dumpster, Melody is placed in witness protection. She is moved out of state, where she falls in love with a minor league baseball player. Her new name, history, and love-life are further complicated by additional moves while awaiting trial.

Dedication

To the three special angels who came into my life:

Avery Callaghan

Alanna Colligan

Ronan Colligan

Your light continues to inspire every page of this book.

Table Of Content

Chapter 1
The Eastern Shore of Maryland

Judge Milligan peered over his glasses and looked directly at me. "What is your plea?"

"Guilty, your honor; however, may I have probation before judgment?"

Judge Milligan's bulging eyeballs spoke first, and then his deep voice echoed around the courtroom, "What!" Perched behind a wall of mahogany and looking down upon me with contempt, he continued, "You want probation before judgment?"

I flinched. His sharp response caught me by surprise. I had previously appeared before this judge on reckless driving and speeding charges, and he seemed so calm and genteel.

"Ms. Vanders, I am *not* a fool! Wasn't that your request last month, and the month before?"

"Uh, yes, your honor."

"Then, with all due respect, you ought to be shaking in your shoes while I'm contemplating the sentence you're about to receive." The judge leaned forward and said, "Without checking the record, I can recall two other times you've appeared here on similar charges."

"Actually," I paused, took a deep breath, and said, "it was three." I quickly counted on my hand, "I mean the four, your honor."

"I stand corrected." Judge Milligan shook his head and then looked down at his paperwork.

"Your honor, I promise, this truly will be the last time."

"And I wish I could believe that," he replied without looking up. "You're twenty-two years of age, which means that by now you should be a better driver than a high school student. It seems to me that you've demonstrated to the State of Maryland that you don't deserve any driving privileges."

"But, your honor, I'm a realtor. I need a driver's license."

I think I struck a raw nerve with the judge.

He looked up from the papers on his desk, removed his glasses, and said, "That, Ms. Vanders, is something you should consider every time you get behind the wheel. Yet, time and time again, you fail to focus on the road and the operation of your vehicle. Quite frankly, your bold request for probation doesn't seem like justice. I ought to put you in jail so our Maryland troopers and local police officers can take it easy for a while." He leaned back in his massive chair in a thoughtful pose. "I tell you what, I'll not revoke your license today, and I'll not put you in jail."

"Thank you, Your Honor." I breathed a little easier. I had considered hiring an attorney to avoid jail time. Whew, saved a little money there. With any luck, the judge would only order a hefty fine as he did the other times I appeared in his courtroom.

"I will, however, suspend your license."

Ouch, I thought, this will hurt my business.

"Perhaps a suspension will teach you not to use gadgets while driving. What exactly was it this time, your cell phone, or your laptop computer?"

"My computer, your honor. I was receiving a signed document, a very critical document on one of my listings. You know the housing market. A signed contract is not easy to get these days."

"Oh, so you're telling me that reading a contract while driving is more important than the public's safety? Ms. Vanders, you don't seem to understand that you have a duty to drive responsibly. That means all your attention should be on the road and on the operation of your vehicle." The judge quieted, shook his head, and began writing something.

His long silence was excruciating. My heart pounded under my blouse as the rest of my body trembled. I was so tense that I broke the shoulder strap on my purse from all my nervous downward pressure, designer handbags shouldn't do that. To calm myself, I took a deep breath, and then without moving my head, I looked around the courtroom in all directions. I could see the tall windows along one side. Above me, there was a large brass chandelier suspended from the soaring ceiling. I looked straight ahead the U.S. and Maryland flags and tried not to stare at anyone item. I wanted to look as if I were giving the judge my full attention.

The judge finally looked up, and my eyes were drawn to his. I exhaled while waiting for his final decision.

"Something tells me, Ms. Vanders, that a ninety-day suspension of your license is not enough, but that's what you shall receive today and you are also ordered to pay a seventeen hundred dollar fine before you leave, and I'm ordering you to take one hundred hours of driving lessons. That means hands-on driving with a certified instructor and classroom time with a strong emphasis on our Maryland laws. Am I clear on this point?"

"Yes, your honor."

"Upon successful completion, you shall have the driving school send the court a letter, and then the State shall return your license, conditionally, that is, because if you show up in my courtroom one more time for even a parking ticket, I'll revoke your license. Do you understand?"

"Yes, your honor."

"Good, then may God grant traveling mercies to all of your real estate clients as you drive them around the county." Judge Milligan picked up his gavel and with a single strike on his desk, he finished my case.

I turned and began to exit the courtroom, but halfway down the center aisle I realized something and turned back toward the judge. Gently raising my hand, I said, "Excuse me, your honor."

"Yes, Ms. Vanders."

"My car, it's parked outside. May I drive it home?"

"Don't test me!" the judge roared.

Frightened by his demeanor, I walked backward toward the rear of the courtroom until my hands felt the metal exit bar on the door. This was not a good day for me.

I proceeded to the cashier's office down the hall. With all of my unhappy experiences in traffic court, I knew the routine quite well. I paid my fine, surrendered my driver's license, and then strode outside, looking for someone to drive me home.

"At least you're not in jail," I said to myself. "Yeah, there is a silver lining!"

Judge Milligan is a tough old bird. I suppose that's good for the drivers on the road, and not so good for drivers like me. With no license, I managed to find someone to take me home. The teenage son of a nearby neighbor who seemed delighted to drive my Mercedes. I handed him my keys, and after we pulled into my driveway, I asked, "What were you doing at the courthouse without a car?"

"I had to hitch a ride to see Judge Milligan. I wrecked my truck and was given a drunk driving citation. That's why I'm glad to see you, Miss Melody, or I wouldn't have a ride home."

"Are you telling me that you're driving on a suspended license?"

"No, not that. The judge revoked it, but said I can apply for a new license again after I graduate from high school."

"Are you drunk now?"

"No, I only had two beers at breakfast, and I can handle that much. Miss Melody, may I give you a word of advice?"

"Sure," I said, as I rolled my eyes.

"You see, I always remembered you with brown hair. Maybe being a blonde isn't such a good idea. Blondes aren't considered too bright, and maybe that influenced Judge Milligan's decision to take your license."

I didn't need to utter another word. The look on my face was convinced the teen to hand me my keys and volunteer to walk the two blocks to his home.

I was about to enter my bungalow, which I inherited after my parents died, when my elderly neighbor Gladys Cutler leaned over her front porch railing and yelled, "Well, Melody, did you lose your driver's license? I bet that'll hurt your real estate business. Maybe you should start looking for another line of work."

I was depressed. Without my driver's license, my real estate income would be severely hampered. Answering the office phones for my broker was one option. I did that job well, thanks to my mother's training, God rest her soul.

When I was much younger, my mother would say, "Melody Doreen Vanders, if you don't cultivate some personality in your conversation, you'll end up working in a dime store." Who ever heard of a dime store? For some reason my southern-belle mother seemed to equate plain personalities with store clerks. I never understood the connection, but I did realize very early in life that I was not suited for retail but real estate, that's my destiny.

Mother thought I needed voice training, so she tried to cultivate a more refined speaking tone and laugh in me, along with some polite casual chatter and good manners. *Be interesting and not self-centered, and don't be blunt, but rather be diplomatic, have a great curiosity in the other person, and most of all* (my father also stressed this last one) *if you want to marry a good man, don't skip church. That's where the best men are found.*

As a young girl, I was quite amused by all the societal conventions of Southern society and preferred watching high society from afar as they demonstrated their perfect politeness. During several parties my parents would host, I much preferred sitting at the top of the stairs and listening below to conversations taking place below, which was some of the most boring twaddle ever created in refined company.

I once overheard someone say, "Gracious, that shy Melody, what will ever become of her?" One would think that was an insult, but it was quickly followed by a charming compliment about my appearance. I found their well-intended whispers amusing because I didn't feel the least bit shy, just careful of my company. They had all misinterpreted my dreamy eyes, which were focused on my imaginary real estate developments and deals of the century. I had a deep desire to succeed in business, make a name for myself, and live out the American dream. Yet I dutifully participated in mother's charm lessons, which also meant being in perpetual training for hostess of the year. *Know the best caterers, stand erect and hold in your stomach, let a pleasant smile be your natural expression, be generous with genuine compliments, listen carefully to others, remember names, set a glorious table, and for goodness's sake, please be more engaged in conversation with short but colorful stories.*

My favorite story concerned a state record which I held. It always irritated Mother, but I found it amusing: No one in the entire State of Maryland had flunked the road test portion of a driver's examination more than I. Eight times in all. That sort of colorful detail was not what she had in mind because no one likes a braggart under any circumstances, despite all the laughs and assorted reactions my personal anecdote always engendered.

I did learn one important life lesson on my ninth driving attempt: *persistence is the key to success.* It worked in obtaining my driver's license, and undoubtedly persistence would help me become a successful realtor, if only I could drive clients around without scaring them half out of their wits. Funny, but I always felt at ease behind the steering wheel, though my passengers never shared my same level of comfort.

From my earliest recollections, I had dreamed of owning a real estate agency and developing beautiful communities. I loved the idea of turning bare fields on the edge of town into charming neighborhoods that would conform to our historic Maryland landscapes and architecture. I visualized lasting residential styles with lavish gardens. They would be smaller, federal-style homes with intimate, colorful yards surrounded by picket fences. I wanted to offer Maryland a handsome alternative to the out of scale McMansions embellished with brick or stone veneers on the street side of the house, making them appear like a woman wearing a designer cocktail dress in the front while exposing her cheap underwear on the backside. They also lacked any measure of landscaping, usually sporting only one lonely sapling in the front yard and a couple of knee-high shrubs around the foundation. In my opinion, they were like warts on the face of our historic small towns.

I never doubted that I would someday achieve my goal of becoming an outstanding Realtor and developer. My plan was so clear in my mind and my desire so overwhelming that I had no interest in the activities of other girls in my high school. While they spent endless hours attending games, parties, and proms, I had enrolled in evening real estate classes. On weekends, I made it a point to learn the market and the basic concepts of good design by visiting area architects and seasoned realtors. After high school graduation, I sat for my real estate exam and became one of the youngest agents in the state.

My next goal was to become a real estate broker and have my own business. *Dream big,* my father had always said. *Dreaming is free, so why not have big dreams?* I wished he could see me now, my father. I do miss him. He was my guiding light.

Shortly after I had obtained my broker's license, I finally qualified to open my own realty company. My trust account had dwindled to just under thirty thousand. Fortunately, I had no mortgage because I needed an office. Commercial space was too expensive for my budget; in fact, it was out of my reach. I could barely afford my Mercedes lease payments even though I had no license to drive, and then there were my ever-escalating insurance premiums, Realtor Board dues, multiple list fees, and my phone bill. I was stretched to the limit (if the truth be told, a little beyond). I certainly couldn't give up my luxurious SUV. My business plan was bare bones yet called for a first-class car to match the name of my new company, *First Class Realty.* With a first-class automobile, I could forgo a fancy office, because I had always made it a policy to pick up my clients from their homes, a public meeting place, or at the municipal Airport. Swank office space didn't seem so important since the latest computer technology allowed my customers to reach me from any location, including my car.

After a house tour of two or three homes, and before I had lost my driver's license, my arrangement was always to drop my clients off at a place of their choosing. On my very bad driving days, they would sternly insist that I stop the car at the next corner. As a courtesy, I'd call for a taxi.

Chapter 2
The Old Gas Station

After two tours in Iraq and many stressful years of intelligence work in the hectic-paced city of Washington, D.C., it was time for Army Lieutenant Colonel Gregory Herman to retire and give his blood pressure a rest. He didn't want to drop completely out of the job market, because he wanted extra spending money to take some grand fishing trips every year, or perhaps buy a mountain cabin near a good fishing stream. Unlike the army, his retirement job had to be a relaxed sort of occupation. So, after signing his final retirement documents with the military, he bought a new Lincoln SUV limousine, believing that chauffeuring people would be that quiet job he needed as a supplement to his military pension.

The Eastern Shore of Maryland had always been Gregory's home until he had joined the service. The last time he returned to the Shore was for his twenty-fifth high school reunion, and it was the last time he saw his former football receiver, Earl Dregs. Gregory never saw Earl again until he purchased an old gas station for his new business. It wasn't just any old station; it was the place where his grandfather was once employed. As a young boy, Gregory would sometimes walk to the station so his grandfather could buy him a Coca-Cola from the vending machine that was kept just inside the garage.

Gregory stood across the street and marveled at his newly purchased station. His emotional ties to the building and its impressive Depression era architecture inspired him to restore the old place. He envisioned how he could string lights under the overhang, showcasing his carefully waxed limo.

The tired structure had been slated for demolition when Gregory purchased it, but he could look beyond its worn-out appearance. To him, it was a proud monument of his childhood, full of fond memories. As he continued to admire his newly acquired property, he pictured an immaculate building with a new red metal roof to replace the existing one. The broken and missing clay tiles served no useful purpose. In fact, they were the cause of a couple rotted rafters that had collapsed into the building. Roof replacement would be his first major project but not the only one. The exterior screamed for new paint, weeds surrounded the foundation walls, and its large picture window in the front was broken. The missing bricks around the top of the flue looked like missing teeth, so Gregory decided to eliminate the flue altogether. These numerous repairs would have to be prioritized to occur over time, but that's exactly what Gregory had, plenty of time.

As he continued to imagine how he would restore the old personal landmark, a shabbily dressed man, who probably smelled as bad as he looked, walked around to the side of the building and urinated.

Gregory shouted from across the street, "Hey, you! Knock that off!" He puffed his chest and darted across the street while thoughts of punching the man permeated his entire being. However, a cooler head prevailed, and his violent thoughts receded.

"What do you think you're doing here?" Gregory pointed to the wet spot on his building.

"Obviously, I'm taking a leak." The man's long, oily, gray locks and beard were a true complement to his soiled and tattered clothes.

"If you need a toilet, use a bathroom." Gregory showed him the two station bathrooms located next to the urine-stained wall. "The doors are open!"

And they were because without hardware, both bathroom doors were leaning against the building.

"I guess you haven't noticed those blackened toilets and sinks!" The bum replied. "You expect me to use those unhealthy things? No way!"

"Let me tell you," Gregory's voice elevated. "You're messing with the wrong owner when you piss on the side of my building!"

"Gregory Herman," the man said as he zipped up his pants. "Did *you* buy this old place? Ha!"

"How do you know my name?"

"I know it, as I've always known it. It's me, Earl. You remember, high school football? At least I was hoping you'd remember." He patted his chest. "Earl Dregs."

"Earl?" Gregory tried to visualize the man behind the mass of matted facial hair that covered the two top buttons of his shirt. He walked around Earl, looking him over. "What happened to you? You're a mess."

"Not a mess, simply retired."

"Retired?" Gregory threw his hands into the air. "From what, Earl, from making bad choices?"

"I was thinking about that the other day."

"You know what, Earl, when you and I were in high school, you were always the better athlete, and you always tried harder. You could out tackle me in football, outrun me in track, but in life, well, I'm surprised you're content with being a bum."

"You got that right. I am content. The booze, the drugs, and a few pills now and then helps my lifestyle."

Gregory rubbed the back of his neck. "I don't understand. Earl, why do you want to live in squalor?"

"It won't be squalor after you fix this place up. I like your old station. It's been my home for a few… uh, maybe several years now, and am I glad you bought it. Hope you didn't pay full price 'cause it could use a little work."

Gregory chuckled. "I don't know if I'll live long enough to make all the needed repairs, but I sorta like the old station."

"Well," Earl's eyes scanned the building. "It's a good place to hang when it rains."

Gregory felt bad. His old friend had obviously fallen on hard times. Even worse, Earl was so delusional that he didn't realize how far he had fallen. Here was an old friend in need, and Gregory felt some obligation to reach out to him. Perhaps helping his old high school friend was his fate, he thought. "Say, Earl, are you hungry?"

"Maybe."

"Would you like to walk up the street with me and get a hotdog? I'm buying."

Earl nodded, and the two headed for the convenience store on the corner.

Chapter 3
My New Office

It was exactly two weeks after completing my hundred hours of driving school when the State of Maryland returned my driver's license. I chose that day to drive through a depressed section of town (Realtors call them *up-and-coming markets*). I spotted a sign out the corner of my eye. Actually, I had taken both eyes off the road and was squinting so I could read the "for rent" sign posted on a 1930s style garage: *$150/mo + utilities*. Although the building was decrepit, it had a fetching new metal roof that resembled red clay tiles. The super low rent gave me an uncontrollable urge to investigate, so without another thought, I cut my wheels left and crossed the double yellow line. That action caused me to collide with a blue sedan, which appeared out of nowhere. The driver of the sedan was furious as his car jumped the curb to avoid other cars. No one was hurt, but the sedan nearly struck a homeless man named Earl, who was "resting" against the very building that piqued my interest.

I got out of my vehicle and managed to get a closer look at the office space while Earl shouted obscenities at me. This was how I met Gregory Herman by accident, *a real accident*. Needless to say, the incident resulted in several more moving violations, whereupon Judge Milligan doubled the fine and suspended my license for three years in lieu of jail time.

The owner, Gregory Herman, was a tall, husky man of about seventy with thinning hair and gray temples. He had been divorced for over fifteen years, and because he had no children or siblings, the army had been his family. A great military colonel he was, but he soon discovered that his limousine business wasn't as lucrative as he had expected, except during high school prom season.

Gregory decided to generate more income by renting out the station's small office and work entirely from the shop area of the building, which was about the size of a residential double garage with a pit. Most of the structural repairs had been completed, including running water in both bathrooms, but nothing had been done to the eight-by-twelve-foot, mildewed office that interested me. The rent included the use of the bathrooms that had temporary plastic *men's* and *women's* signs pasted on the doors.

I was so happy to find an affordable space, and I didn't mind moving a chair every time I wanted to pull out a filing cabinet drawer. I did have a big picture window that looked out onto the busy street, the owner's limo, and the back of Earl's head. On the downside, the building had no heat, and the lavatories had never felt the stiff bristles of a toilet bowl brush. There were also some spindly weeds growing up through the cracked concrete floor, no doubt nourished overtime by faulty plumbing. Two sturdy masonry pillars in the front supported an overhang where automobiles once parked for a fill-up, the antique pumps long ago removed. Most of all, it had the only outdoor spigot, which offered Gregory a shady place to wash, wax, and display his beautiful black limo under the massive lighted overhang.

My previous broker was surprised to learn that I had rented an office in such a blighted area, but Gregory and I understood the potential of the building. We also discovered a wonderful unintended consequence of our landlord-tenant relationship. I had no choice but to turn in my leased Mercedes after Judge Milligan suspended my license, so I decided to use Gregory's services to chauffeur my clients. He never seemed to have much to do each day after polishing his limo, so for the first time he had a regular customer, me.

Gregory charged by the hour for his services and forgave me several months of rent because I had paid a contractor to make the bathrooms usable. I also insulated and installed a heating and air conditioning system in my office. After my all my debts were paid, including the excessive court costs, I was in no position to spend money frivolously. One could say that I had put the word "broke" in real estate broker.

Overall, my business relationship with Gregory worked well, because his customers generally needed a chauffeur during the dinner hours when my office was closed, although occasionally we would need to coordinate scheduling when a wedding would interrupt my Saturday house tours. Soon both of our businesses began to grow as did our friendship. Even Earl began to warm up to me somewhat. He finally allowed Gregory to give him a military style shave and a haircut, and I gave Earl all of my father's clothes that I hadn't given to the Good Will.

Chapter 4
The Contact at Baltimore Airport

Gregory's office turned out to be a blessing for me. I had worked at this location for just over a year when I got an interesting international phone call.

"Good afternoon, First Class Realty, Melody Vanders speaking."

The gentleman on the line claimed he was from Mexico City and said his name was Dr. Gonzales. I believed him, though his accent sounded more Russian than Mexican. The doctor needed a small home to rent for a year with an option to renew. Although my rental business was usually quite time consuming with little financial reward, one of my best clients owned a guest cottage that would be perfect for Mr. Gonzales and his wife to rent. It was located on a waterfront farm. Dr. Gonzales said he would be working on some research documents, mostly from home. The cottage was in very good condition and completely furnished, making it ideal for the doctor and his wife. I worked out the particulars over the phone, and to cinch the deal I agreed to rent a storage facility to receive many of his belongings ahead of his move to America.

Over the next several weeks, I corresponded frequently with Dr. Gonzales, who wanted verification that every crate and box from Mexico had arrived and was properly stored and they were. The doctor was always pleasant and gentlemanly. I distinctly remembered my last phone conversation with him. It was the day before his flight was to arrive. He was upbeat and quick-witted, while giving me the necessary flight information, explaining that his wife needed to take care of some last-minute details in Mexico City and would join him later.

I informed Dr. Gonzales that I would meet him at the Baltimore airport and would hold up a sign displaying his name. For easy identification, the doctor said that he would be wearing a dark blue suit and a yellow tie. We agreed that I would take him directly to his hotel, and on the following day, I planned to show him the rental cottage and have him sign the lease. Gregory and I would help the doctor with his initial errands until he could lease a car. The doctor was quite impressed with our plan and our willingness to help him upon his arrival to America. Performing these extra duties was always costly, but quality service often produced future clients when they were ready to purchase a home.

I looked out my office window and saw Gregory waiting in his limousine. He had placed my magnetic *First Class Realty* signs on the sides of his limo. This pleased me because I wanted Dr. Gonzales to have a great first impression of my business.

The limo's headlights cast a long beam, which allowed me to see the fall leaves swirling in the air. I chuckled as some landed on the hood of his freshly washed automobile. Gregory honked his horn.

"I'm coming," I yelled as I poked my head out the front door. I grabbed my purse, a light coat, and waited patiently as my computer printed out an extra-large sheet of paper that said in bold letters: *Dr. Gonzales.*

After locking the office, I hopped in the front seat. "Don't worry. We're not late. I checked, and the flight is running a little behind schedule. But then, on the other hand, it wouldn't hurt to step on it. We can never tell if traffic on the Chesapeake Bay Bridge will be slow or stopped."

As we neared the airport, I looked up in the sky and saw a plane with its landing lights on. "Gregory, that's it! I bet that's his plane. You must hurry, or we'll miss Dr. Gonzales when he arrives."

"Calm down, Melody. That could be anybody's plane. All sorts of planes are constantly coming in for a landing. May I remind you that I have been ready for over an hour, and it was you who delayed our departure?"

"Okay, okay! So maybe the flight isn't as late as I thought, and maybe that jet isn't the right one, but we can't miss him. I want to meet him as soon as he steps off his plane."

Gregory increased his speed and drove up to the *Arrivals* terminal, where no spaces available to park.

"I don't believe it! Gregory." I panicked, as usual. "We'll have to double or triple-park."

"Melody, are you crazy? You want me to park in the middle of the road and block terminal traffic when the airport police are everywhere?"

"Really now! You can trust me to move your limo a few feet if I'm approached by any police officers."

"Oh, no you don't!" Gregory gave me this awful look. "You should go inside and find the doctor, and I'll take care of my vehicle."

"Okay, you win." I started to walk away when I heard Gregory's voice shouting, "The sign! Don't forget the sign."

I turned back and snatched the sign from his hand.

"And, Melody, don't forget, Dr. Gonzales is wearing a dark blue suit and a yellow tie."

"All right, all right," I yelled back.

The seconds seemed like hours as I looked for Dr. Gonzales. I found a prominent place to stand so that all arriving passengers could see my sign. I finally spotted a man wearing a dark blue suit and a yellow tie.

"Dr. Gonzales?"

"Yes, and you must be Ms. Vanders."

"Yes, sir, I sure am." I tucked the sign in my designer hobo purse, leaving it somewhat open, and pointed to the *baggage claim* sign. "This way, Doctor, to the luggage carousel."

"No need, I only have this one carry-on."

"Good, because I'm in a bit of a hurry."

"What's the problem?"

"We're double parked, and I'm worried that the authorities will complain before we can leave."

"Authorities?"

As we walked past several kiosks and stores, I noticed the doctor's forehead dripping with sweat. He stopped suddenly.

"Melody, I believe we are being followed."

"Followed?" Hmm, this sort of thing only happens in the movies.

"Melody, please," with a tremor in his voice the doctor said, "Listen carefully as we continue to walk. I dropped a thumb drive into your purse. Give it to no one except my wife. Can you do that for me?"

"I promise."

"Good. She will be arriving tomorrow."

"What's going on?"

"I want you to give the thumb drive to my wife, because she knows what to do with it. There is information on that thumb drive that certain companies want destroyed. That also goes for the items I had shipped to your office. I trust that they are securely stored."

"Yes, Doctor, they are, but I don't understand."

"You will. My name is actually Ivan Morozov. My wife is from Mexico, and I often use her last name, Gonzales, because we live in Mexico most of the time." The doctor squeezed my arm as he spoke. "The information you possess in your purse is a lifesaving antidote to be administered to those who have been infected with a lethal bioweapon." Pulling me along, he continued. "Melody, make it look like you're glad to see me smile."

I wiped the fear from my face and looked up at the doctor as if I had just heard the silliest story.

"The manufacturer of the bioweapon wants my life and my work destroyed to protect their insidious desire to reduce the population, and I have no doubt that they have hired hitmen to find me."

We walked past a few more shops, and then suddenly a man in a dark overcoat grabbed the doctor from behind.

"Ivan." The man said with sinister force.

"Get your hands off of me." The doctor reacted with equal force. What do you want?"

"I believe, you know Doctor Morozov."

A second man appeared dressed in a dark suit, and the two continued to manhandle the doctor. I'll never forget their faces. They both looked like pure evil, and I found it odd that bystanders were not interested in the commotion as the doctor was escorted away in a rough manner. It seemed as though the passengers were more interested in getting to their gates on time than helping a man being mistreated by thugs.

"Run! Melody, run," the doctor shouted over his shoulder.

And I did, in the opposite direction. I ran as fast as I could, passing people on my left and right. I even dashed down the escalator and out to the curb to Gregory's limo. I didn't see him, so I hopped in the driver's seat, placed my foot on the brakes, and pressed the *start* button on the dash.

"Oh, dear, where are you, Gregory, when I need you the most," I cried as I pulled away from the curb, barely missing the car in front of me. My braking action jerked Gregory awakes, who was snoozing on the back seat.

"Melody, what are you doing? You just hit that guy's bumper!"

"It was close, but I missed it."

"Melody! There's convenience store up ahead. Pull into their parking lot and let me drive!"

I did manage to park the limo without incident to Gregory's great relief.

Gregory got behind the wheel and asked, "Where's the doctor?"

We had a ninety-minute drive home from the Baltimore airport, seventy if I were driving, but it was enough time to explain what just happened.

As we crossed over the Bay Bridge, Gregory insisted that I call the FBI, so I did. I gave the agent on the call my name, address, and phone number and told him my story. The agent had some interest in the case after I told him that I believed the doctor was in mortal danger. I even got the feeling that he took careful notes, but the issue didn't seem to be a top priority to the FBI, or maybe that's how they normally react.

After Gregory dropped me off at my place, I sank into my favorite living room chair and realized that my supposedly profitable real estate day, turned out to be a whirlwind of surprise, intrigue, and financial disappointment for my business.

Chapter 5
The Dumpster in Annapolis

I didn't expect the FBI to come calling anytime soon, but they did, in the wee hours of the morning at my home. The sun nowhere to be seen when my doorbell rang. With my eyes not fully opened, I quickly donned my bathrobe and slippers and peeked through the curtains.

When I opened my front door, as far as my door chain would allow, two FBI agents, a male and a female, presented me with credentials, so I invited them inside, but the male agent returned to their government car. I told the female agent that I couldn't speak to anyone until I had at least one cup of coffee. She obliged.

"I am sorry to have interrupted your sleep," the female agent said, "but I'm here because we've located Dr. Ivan Morozov. His body was found in a dumpster behind a busy Annapolis restaurant."

"Oh dear! Tell me that's not true."

"His neck was broken, and he had several bruises on his face and body. We presume he was tortured before he was murdered."

"That's awful, but how did you know it was the doctor's body?"

"His passport was in the chest pocket of his suit. The picture and body matched, but that's not all we found. Your business card was also found in his coat, and a second one on top of his body."

"Oh, dear, my business card has my photo on it!"

"How many cards did you give the doctor?"

"I don't know. I usually place a couple on all my correspondence. I wrote to him a few times to his Mexico address because his email wasn't so reliable. He could have had several of my business cards."

My coffee was ready, so I poured myself a cup, sank down into my favorite living room chair, and watched the agent take notes. "I suspected the doctor was in mortal danger, because as soon as the two men forced him away, he told me to run."

"Can you describe the men?"

"Yes, but everything happened so fast. I got the best look at the first guy, and I'll never forget him. He was a white man, tall, about six foot-three with a husky build. His black hair was thick, and he had a high forehead. Oh, he was mean looking with a huge jawline someone that I would not want to meet in an elevator."

"Anything else?"

"He had dark eyes and dark, furry eyebrows."

"And the second man?"

"He was a big man, too, with light brown hair with an old-fashioned flat-top haircut. That's all I had time to notice."

"Melody, would you be able to recognize him again?"

"Absolutely."

"Allow me to explain why we're here," the female agent said. "We want you to be very vigilant and pay attention to your surroundings. If you suspect your life is in danger at any time, you are to call this number. We'll then make arrangement with the U.S. Marshals to have you picked up immediately."

"Why would anyone want to threaten me?"

"We don't know exactly why, but your doctor friend was undoubtably tortured to gain information, information that those men probably suspect that you might have."

Of course, I had the info, but I was determined to turn all the documents and thumb drive over to the doctor's wife, as promised. I knew the information contained an important anecdote, and to lock it away in some evidence locker may put people's lives in jeopardy.

"Ms. Vanders, it's obvious that the doctor did reveal your identity and your location to the two perpetrators."

"Eee-gads! I never gave Doctor Morozov my home address, but he certainly had my name, work address, and cellphone number. It's all on my business card. What should I do in the meantime?"

"I'm glad you asked," the agent said. She paused for a few moments while looking directly into my eyes. "I want you to pack a go-bag with all your overnight necessities, just the basics including any meds you would need, and one day's clothing, no more. We'll keep it in our possession. Should we need to whisk you away on a moment's notice, you will have one day's essentials. If we can't get you immediately, the local Sheriff will dispatch someone."

"That means you want me to pack now?"

"Yes, Ms. Vanders. If you should ever need us, we don't want you to waste time packing when your life could be in danger. We may even ask you to meet us at a separate location for your safety."

"And then what?"

"That all depends on the situation."

I packed my go-bag, gave it the agent, and we said our goodbyes.

It was still early, and Gregory wouldn't be around until eight, so I went back to bed.

Chapter 6
Breakfast in Melody's Kitchen

Later, I woke up to some heavy banging in my kitchen. After my earlier meeting with the FBI, the noise would have scared me to death, except I also heard Gregory's mellow tenor voice singing, *Oh, What a Beautiful Morning*.

Earl and Gregory ate all their meals at a fast-food restaurant or a local diner, so I had invited them to use my kitchen for their morning meal as long as they would cook breakfast for me, too. This was their first attempt.

I quickly dressed and walked out to the kitchen.

"Good morning, Melody. Coffee?" Gregory said with a cheerful voice.

"Yes, please." I looked around the kitchen and saw that nearly all the dishes from the cupboards were piled along the counters.

"Melody," Earl said, "if you're going to invite us to fix breakfast, at least tell us where you keep your frying pans."

"Oh, that would be inside the oven."

"Thanks. You sure do keep a clean house."

"I'm glad you approve, Earl, but I never expected you to notice *clean*."

"Oh, yes, I notice those things, just like I noticed that you're almost out of eggs."

"Well, when Gregory drives me to the market, I'll buy a couple dozen. Anything else?"

"Yes, I'd like you to pick out a nice big ham, butt portion, please." Gregory chimed in.

"Don't worry, it's on my list, but Earl, Gregory, I have something more important to talk about other than a butt ham and eggs. The FBI came knocking on my door before sunrise."

"That's not good," Earl said

"Fellas, the FBI believes that my life could be in danger."

"Wow, that's really no good," Earl said.

"They told me they found Doctor Gonzales's a.k.a. Dr. Ivan Morozov's dead body."

"Body? Ouch, doubly not good," Earl said.

"That's not all. It appears that he was tortured before he was murdered."

"Now, why would they do a thing like that?" Earl asked.

"Oh, Earl, think!" Gregory said. "They probably wanted to find out who met the doctor at the airport. Don't you see, Melody can identify those two thugs, and they probably will want to know if the doctor passed any information to Melody."

"And did he?" Earl asked.

"Well, yes, a thumb drive, but I didn't tell the FBI, because the doctor wanted his wife to have it. After all, it's their property."

"I'm proud of you for not telling the Feds," Earl said. "You just can't trust the FBI these days. Not that I could ever trust cops."

"Earl! That's the wrong attitude," Gregory said. "Keeping the Feds out of the loop about the thumb drive was not wise."

"Gregory, I made him a promise to the doctor to surrender his research only to his wife. Mrs. Gonzales will be arriving soon, and I'll turn everything over to her. After all, with her husband dead, she's now the sole and rightful owner. The documents are obviously important." Thinking about the mess I was in, I plopped down in a kitchen table chair. "This entire Gonzales thing has put me in a position that I don't like."

"Now what will you do?" Earl asked.

"Melody!" Gregory gave me a stern look. "If the men you saw in the airport tortured the doctor in order to get these materials, don't think for a moment they won't do the same to you. So, I'm asking you this. What will you do if they should show up on your doorstep?"

"And my answer to you is, I don't know what I would do if they should show up, probably freeze."

Earl shrugged. "Gee, Melody, all you need to do is tell the bad guys that you don't have the doctor's gadget, reports, or luggage."

"Earl!" Gregory gave him a sour look. "Think this through. It's serious."

"There is a backup plan." Melody held up a business card. "The FBI gave me an emergency number to call if I feel I'm in danger."

"Then get out a black *Sharpie* and write that number on the inside of your cell phone case. You should also write it in an address book under Floyd B. Insley in case you lose your phone."

Earl laughed and slapped the countertop. "Oh, I get it Floyd B. Insley is FBI, clever."

Just then the doorbell rang. "I'll get it," Earl said, as he dashed toward the front door. "Maybe it's the bad guys! I want to meet these thugs." He peered out the window in the front door.

"Who is it, Earl?" I asked.

"Oh, it's just an old lady, bent over and holding onto a walker."

Melody threw down her napkin. "Earl, how could you be so insensitive? That's Mrs. Cutler, my next-door neighbor and cleaning lady."

"Cleaning lady who uses a walker?" Gregory held back a laugh.

"Yes, cleaning lady. On my mother's deathbed, I promised her that I would keep Gladys on as our housekeeper. And now, four years later, it means, she eats whatever she wants and dusts the two coffee tables in the living room, all for twenty-five dollars a week." I went to the front door, pushed Earl aside, and smiled. "Come on in, Gladys. How are you feeling today?"

"Oh, my lumbago is bothering me, but not so much that I can't work for you today. I was planning on making that apple pie I promised you, but the way I'm feeling, it's not going to happen."

"Thank you for the thought, Gladys. It's very sweet of you."

"You're welcome." She sauntered into the kitchen, carefully maneuvering her walker, poured herself a cup of coffee, and sat down at the kitchen table. "I saw you had the FBI come to your door in the middle of the night. Is there something you're not telling me, Melody?"

"Now, that's pretty smart of you," Earl said. "How'd you know they were FBI?"

"I've watched enough TV in my day to recognize them anywhere."

"Excuse me, Gladys, this is Earl Dreggs and Gregory Herman. Gregory is my office landlord, and Earl, well, he's just Earl."

"Nice to meet you, both."

"Gladys, Earl and Gregory have agreed to make breakfast for me every morning."

"Then put another egg on for me. I like mine over easy on a piece of toast. Better let Gregory do the cooking. I don't like the look of Earl's grubby fingernails." Gladys turned away from Gregory and Earl and looked me squarely in the eyes. "Okay, Melody, cough it up. What did the G-Men want?"

"They came to tell me that my life is in danger."

"What?" Gladys's eyes widened and her back straightened as much as her arthritis would allow. "How can that be?"

"There were these two men whom I saw at the airport when Gregory and I went to pick up my client."

"Did you see them, Gregory?"

"No, ma'am."

"He fortunately was in his limo while I went inside the terminal. Gladys, I watched these men manhandle my client before they forced him out of the terminal. What's more, Gladys, they murdered him and stuck him in a dumpster."

"Do these evil doers know where you live and work?"

"Maybe, I sure hope not, but if they do, it means I could be placed in a witness protection program."

Gladys took my hand. "Melody, what are you going to do? What am I going to do? If you go into witness protection, I'll lose my cleaning job."

"In the meantime, I'm going to work at my office. Gregory and Earl will be there, and I'll have to see what happens next."

Gregory chimed in, "Miss Gladys, you should go home. Hanging around here could put your life in danger if these men should show up at this house."

"Well, okay, but what about my breakfast and my twenty-five dollars?"

I grabbed my purse and gave Gladys her money for services rendered, sort of.

Chapter 7
The Call from Atlanta

I just sat down at my office desk when my cell phone rang.

"Your phone is ringing," Gregory said. "And remember, the FBI is probably listening in on your calls.

It was Mrs. Gonzales, or so she claimed.

"Mrs. Gonzales, who is Ivan Morozov?" I asked.

"He is my husband. How did you know his true name?"

"He told me."

"Ms. Vanders, I am worried because Ivan hasn't called me to say he arrived safely. I just arrived in Atlanta from Mexico City, and I'm now boarding the plane to Baltimore. Have you heard from my husband, and have you secured our research?"

"Oh, yes, Mrs. Gonzales, and I must tell you something important. When you arrive in Baltimore, go directly to the Bay Shuttle. Tell the driver that you want to get off at the Hyatt here on the Eastern Shore. I'll reserve a shuttle seat for you and a room at the hotel. Both the shuttle and the hotel room will be under my name, Melody Vanders. Got that?

"Yes, Ms. Vanders, but I fear something is very wrong. I can tell by your voice."

"That's all I can say for now." I stopped the call at that point and took a deep breath. I didn't want to say anything more.

"Gregory! Gregory! I yelled into the shop area.

"Hold your horses, Melody."

"Mrs. Gonzalas just called. She just boarded a plane in Atlanta and will be arriving soon in Baltimore. I told her to take the Bay Shuttle as soon as she arrives in Baltimore, and that I'll reserved a seat for her under my name."

"*Your* name?"

"Well, it's my credit card."

"Melody, those professional hitmen could have hacked into Maria Gonzales's phone and will be looking for her inside that airport terminal or at the Hyatt. If they've been hired by some big corporation, they will have the means and the money to do just that. Don't you see? Asking Maria to wander around looking for the Bay Shuttle could put her life in danger."

"Oh, Gregory, I didn't think of that! It means we need to meet Mrs. Gonzales the second her plane arrives just in case the bad guys are waiting for her."

"Melody, you need to call the FBI. In the meantime, I have no chauffeuring jobs today, so I'm available."

"Thanks, Gregory, Mrs. Gonzales is the only one who knows what to do with the doctor's research. We can't put her life in danger."

"Then grab your purse and hop in my limo."

"But first, I need you to take me to the Hyatt, so I can make a reservation and get the room key.

"That means we'll need a female decoy to take the Bay Shuttle to the Hyatt under your name."

"Gregory! That's nearly impossible because we need this woman today!"

There was a slight pause as Gregory and I thought, and then together we said, "Gladys Cutler!"

"I'll call her right now, and we'll meet her at her house after we get a room at the Hyatt."

Gladys was surprised to see Gregory and me as she opened her door.

"May we come in?" I asked.

"Something extremely important has come up," Gregory chimed in. "Melody and I need to discuss it with you."

After we sat down in her living room, I asked Gladys, "Have you ever spent the night at the Hyatt Resort Hotel?"

"Now, why would I do a fool thing like that when I have a perfectly nice home right here?"

"Oh, for room service and a fancy meal," I said. "You've always said you wished you could go someplace to be pampered."

"I don't consider three miles up the highway going anywhere."

"Let me explain," Gregory said. "We need you to be a decoy."

"Like an undercover spy? Gladys said.

"Sort of," Gregory said. "It means it could put you in danger. I'll drive you and Earl to the Baltimore Airport, where your passage on the Bay Shuttle has been paid by Melody Vanders. From there, you'll take the shuttle with Earl to the Hyatt here in town and spend the night. Here is the room key."

"Spend the night with Earl? I wouldn't mind spending the night with a man, but not that man. Have you seen his fingernails? I could plant strawberries under his cuticles."

"Earl's only job is to make sure you arrive safely to your room," Gregory said. "We don't want him to appear like he's travelling with you, but merely look like a kind person helping an elderly lady. It's all undercover work."

"I'd be like a private detective!" Gladys perked up. "I think I'll wear my wig and large frame glasses."

"That means you'll do it?" I asked.

"Of course, it's better than sitting around and watching my soaps. Besides, an old gal like me needs a little excitement now and then." Gladys left the room briefly and returned wearing a blonde wig and large wide framed glasses. "How do I look?"

"Believe me," I said. "No one will recognize you."

We all agreed to Gladys's disguise because no one knew what Mrs. Gonzales actually looked like. Besides, at this point, whatever Gladys wants, Gladys gets. We desperately needed her help.

"Now that Gladys has agreed to be our decoy," Gregory said, "I'm sure Earl will cooperate. It sounds like it's all settled. All we need to do now is be at the airport on time."

Chapter 8
The Bay Shuttle

We arrived at the Baltimore-Washington-Thurgood Marshall Airport a half-hour before Mrs. Gonzalez's arrival time. Gregory parked along the curb in the arriving passenger section. Not wanting to be recognized, I put on Gregory's chauffer's cap and sunglasses and hopped in the front seat behind the wheel.

"Gladys, you better hang on to my arm," Earl said, "while I carry your walker. In fact, I'll get a wheelchair for you." The two went inside the terminal and headed to the Bay Shuttle's waiting room.

Gregory held a small sign close to his chest that said *Gonzales,* making sure that only deplaning passengers could read it. Soon, a middle-aged woman approached Gregory.

"I'm Mrs. Gonzales; where's Melody?"

"She's waiting for us in my limo," Gregory said.

"Okay, I shall trust you, but please call me Maria. I want you to know that a very menacing man followed me to the airport in Mexico City."

"Did you see him on your flight?"

"I couldn't tell. I was in first class and didn't see any second-class passengers."

"Then we must hurry for your safety. Just one bag?"

"Yes, my carry-on."

"Good." Gregory took Maria's arm and her bag and looked around the area for a suspicious-looking man but saw no one fitting that description. "Whoever this thug was, let's hope that he wasn't looking for you."

Unfortunately, Maria requested to use the restroom, which frustrated Gregory. As he stood waiting, he made a call to Earl, checking to see if he and Gladys were in the Bay Shuttle waiting room.

"Earl, has the shuttle arrived?"

"Yes, it just pulled up."

While waiting for Maria, Gregory spotted a man who fit the description of a menacing thug. He noticed that his eyes were franticly looking around the terminal as if in search of someone.

"Earl, get Gladys on that bus now. There's a suspicious person hanging around, and I suspect he's looking for Mrs. Gonzalez."

"Gregory, two G-Men just flashed their badges to the driver before boarding the Shuttle. What should I do?"

"Act natural, board the bus, and get Gladys to the Hyatt. If they are FBI, that's a good thing."

Gregory looked at his watch while he kept a watchful eye on the person of interest. He called Melody. "Melody, it's possible that a hitman is here in the terminal looking for Mrs. Gonzalez."

"Oh, dear, I was afraid of that. Can you tell if Floyd B. Insley is hanging around?"

"It's impossible to tell because most passengers are all dressed like federal agents, but the good news is Earl and Gladys are boarding the Bay Shuttle."

As Gladys found a seat on the bus, Earl stood outside with the driver and gave him their names. "I'm Earl Dreggs, and that elderly lady is Melody Vander's guest."

The G-Men were seated near the door, and their ears perked up when they heard the name Melody Vanders.

"I see," said the driver. "Am I right that you both are to be dropped off at the Hyatt?"

"Yeah, but it's only a coincidence that I'm with that old broad," Earl said. "You see, she ain't with me. I'm just helping her out 'cause she uses a walker."

"I'll put that walker in the back for now," the bus driver said. "And when we arrive at your destination, I'll hand it back."

The G-man seated nearest the door gave his fellow officer a wink and a nod, and then they both hopped off the bus.

As the Bay Shuttle pulled away from the airport, Earl looked out the rear window and saw no one tailing them, but he did see one of the G-Men making a call. He breathed a sigh of relief, believing it was a clean getaway for now.

In the meantime, Gregory escorted Mrs. Gonzales down the escalator and out the front doors of the terminal to his limo. He took over the driver's seat, and I hopped in the back with Maria.

"Was there any trouble?' I asked.

"No," Gregory said. "Perhaps only a false alarm when Mrs. Gonzales saw a suspicious-looking man."

"Do you have the things that we shipped?" Maria asked.

"Yes, look over your shoulder," I said. "Behind this seat, it's all there."

Maria was greatly relieved as she looked at the two crates that were previously shipped to me. She closed her eyes and crossed herself as if a prayer were answered. Maria explained that the crates contained all of Ivan's hard copies of his work and original lab reports.

"Well then, mission almost accomplished," Gregory said. "Next stop, the rental cottage."

"You haven't told me about Ivan."

I grabbed Maria's hand. "We kept this information from you for your own safety. When Ivan arrived in Baltimore, and as the doctor and I walked down the airport corridor, he was overpowered by two large men. They whisked him away and murdered him."

"No doubt, hired assassins," Gregory said.

Maria looked away and leaned on the window, sobbing quietly. After she composed herself, she said, "I always knew there was much trouble in his line of work, and I suspected danger by the tone of your voice on the phone." Maria located a tissue in her purse and dabbed her nose. "Ivan was murdered because of his discoveries. All of Ivan's work, including his conclusions, can be found in those crates and on his thumb drive."

"I have it with me," I said.

Maria looked at me with relief.

I began to dig in my purse until I found the thumb drive. "Here, Maria, I never liked being in charge of this thing."

"You are quite wise, Melody. However, as long as I have Ivan's documents, I could be their next target."

"Melody, you must keep the thumb drive, so a second copy is available."

"She can't keep it," Gregory said. "As a friend, I feel she's already too deep in this situation."

"Very well." Maria took the thumb drive and handed Gregory a piece of paper. "I need to go to this address outside of Washington, D.C. It's a safe house. I was instructed to go there if anything ever happened to my husband. Tomorrow morning I'll turn my husband's documents over to the Department of Health and Human Services."

Chapter 9
Room Service at the Hyatt Resort

At the Hyatt Resort, Earl escorted Gladys directly to her room. "Mrs. Cutler, do you have your room key?"

She handed it to Earl, who demonstrated how to unlock the door.

"Mrs. Cutler, from now on, remember you are only Gladys Cutler."

"Do I look like I have bats in my belfry? Of course, I'm Gladys Cutler." Gladys stepped inside the room, turned around and said with firm authority, "This is goodbye, Earl, but I thank you for your help."

"How will you get home, Miss Gladys?"

"I'll be fine. Melody gave me cab fare."

Earl set Gladys's overnight bag just inside the door.

"Thank you, Earl." Gladys closed the door. She looked at herself in the full-length mirror, removed her blonde wig, massaged her head, and smiled.

Moments later she heard a knock at the door and a voice saying, "Room Service."

She opened the door, and a waiter carrying a tray entered. "Shall I put the food and tea on your table?"

"Of course. I wouldn't want it on the floor."

Lifting the cloche, "A charcuterie board for your pleasure, Ma'am, and a pot of hot tea. A gift from Melody Vanders."

40

Impressed by the service and the food, Gladys said, "Oh, my, doesn't that beat all." She reached into her coin purse and handed him a quarter.

"Thank you, ma'am," the waiter said in a cheerful voice, but he grimaced once he was down the corridor and out of sight.

A short time later, and after Gladys sampled a few items and poured herself a cup of tea, there was another knock on the door. When she opened the door, two men entered, showing their badges.

"We're FBI, and we have a few questions for you, Mrs. Gonzales."

Gladys immediately noticed that they were not the same agents she saw in Baltimore when boarding the bus. "I'm sorry, you're mistaken. I'm Gladys Cutler. I can show you my ID card issued by the State of Maryland."

"No, thank you." The agent could clearly see that the white haired and wrinkled Gladys, who needed a walker, was not the middle-aged Maria Gonzales. "However, we do want to know why you're in this room."

"Well, it's like this. My next-door neighbor, Melody Vanders, paid for the room for a real estate client of hers. Melody's a broker. Anyway, lucky for me, the client didn't show, and because the room was paid for, I'm here as my neighbor's fortunate guest."

"Ma'am, do you know Maria Gonzales?"

"No, I never met or spoke with her."

"Do you mind if we have a look around?"

"Help yourselves, and won't you join me for a few snacks and some hot tea? The hotel gave me more than I could eat, and they laid it out so beautifully."

"No, thank you." Satisfied that there were no other occupants in the room, the agents left.

Chapter 10
The Washington Safe House

Gregory and I made it to the safe house in D.C. without incident, and after leaving Maria and her things at the safe house, we headed back to the Eastern Shore.

While in the limo, Gregrory said with great pleasure, "Melody, we plotted and executed a remarkable plan to get Mrs. Gonzales to safety, and we did it with military precision."

It was nice to hear, but both of us realized that there could be more trouble on the horizon.

Just after ten-thirty, while Gregory and I were nearly home, my cellphone rang. As I reached into my purse for my phone, the thumb drive fell out. "Oh, no! I can't believe it!"

"What?" Gregory said.

I handed him the thumb drive, and he snapped back, "Oh, no!"

"Oh, yes, Gregory. Maria managed to slip it back into my purse."

The call on my cellphone was from the Hyatt. Gladys wanted to go home and sleep in her own bed. I insisted she use the cab fare and suspected that Gladys wanted to keep the money and hoodwink us into driving her home.

"I'm sorry, Gladys. Gregrory and I are worn out, so please take a cab." I didn't tell her it was a trip to D.C., nor did I mention our side trip to D.C., but nevertheless, she agreed to take the taxi.

The following morning, Gladys came for breakfast at my house. She spent nearly half hour at the kitchen sink scrubbing Earl's fingernails with a fine brush, while Gregory and I discussed the thumb drive. We had a passing thought that we should mail it to the D.C. address where we dropped off Mrs. Gonzales but knowing that the information contained on the drive was so critical, we scratched that plan and decided to wait until we heard from her.

"Well," Gladys said. "Yesterday was quite exciting. What's our next adventure?"

Chapter 11
Out of Business

Two days later, I felt on top of the world, at least the first half of the day was marvelous. November often has a few warm days, and this day was a perfect sweater-weather day. I had just closed two real estate deals. Earl brought in the mail and showed me that my commission checks had arrived, over twenty-five thousand dollars. Gregory spotted me dancing around my tiny office, waving my two checks that represented the greatest week of my career.

"It appears that your business just got a huge boost," Gregory said.

Earl's tone seemed a bit philosophic. "Well, Melody, it's like this. I don't want you to get too excited over your new found riches."

Gregory butted in, "Earl! "Don't spoil Melody's happiness. Let her bask in this success. What could it hurt?"

Earl gave Gregory a serious negotiating stare. "I think it's time to up your office rental rates, Gregory. That limo schtick has caught on with Melody's business. Come on, Melody, toss some more green Gregory's way and share the wealth. For that matter, I helped out yesterday, too."

"You know, Earl, you're right. I do need to pay Gregory more, and I should pay you something, as well."

"Now, Melody, don't take this wrong," Earl said. "It was just a suggestion."

"And a good one, too," I said.

I got out my checkbook and wrote both men a handsome check."

I endorsed my commission checks *for deposit only* and handed them to Gregory to place into my account at the bank. "Here, now we're square. Just make sure you deposit my commission checks before cashing yours." I was then interrupted by a phone call. "First Class Realty, Melody Vanders speaking."

The voice on the phone said, "We're Federal Marshals Berg and Robinson, and we're heading to your office. The two of us have been assigned to your case. Do not leave your office or answer any more phone calls. Just stay put until we get there."

I was dumbfounded as the call ended without even a goodbye.

"Gregory, Earl, you can't leave me. That call was from Federal Marshals."

Gregory's eyes widened.

"The man on the phone said he was a Federal Marshal. Gregory, hold off on the bank deposits. I need you to stay with me. The feds are heading to this office, and I'm not to answer the phone, and he also said that I'm to stay put until they come."

"Then I'll wait in the men's room," Earl said, as he grabbed a magazine from my desk. "It sounds like trouble."

Half an hour later, two U.S. Marshals arrived. They showed me their credentials, Marshals Maggie Berg and Bill Robinson. I immediately asked for the two FBI agents whom I first met.

"They are on their way, Ms. Vanders. Let me explain," Marshal Berg said. "My partner and I will be escorting you to your new residence."

"New residence? What residence?" I asked. "Can Gregory stay and hear all of this?"

"Yes," Marshal Robinson said, "because we know Gregory Herman was involved with transporting Maria Gonzales to Washington. Marshal Robinson looked at Gregory with a most serious stare. "Mr. Herman, should you ever feel at any time that your life is in danger, you are to contact this number immediately." He handed Gregory a business card.

"So, what's going on?" Gregory asked.

"Several hours ago, the D.C. police got a call from a man who heard loud, violent screams coming from his next-door neighbor's house. The police were dispatched immediately. According to the caller, once the sirens got close, two men dashed out of his neighbor's house, one man carried a file crate. When the local police arrived, they found the body of Maria Gonzales lying in the living room. They also discovered the two homeowners bound and gagged in the kitchen. The female was strangled and the male near death, but he was able to tell the officers that Maria's neck was snapped after she had handed over the crate."

"Does that mean the thugs got the reports?" Gregory asked.

"Apparently not," Marshal Robinson explained. "With his last few breaths, the homeowner said that after his neighbor called and reported two suspicious men prowling around their house, Mrs. Gonzales insisted on burning all the reports in their fireplace and refill one of the file crates with reams of scratch paper to give it weight. When the murderers broke into the house, they didn't know the reports had all been destroyed with the help of kerosene from an oil lamp on the mantle. The male victim never gave a description of the two men and died before the paramedics arrived."

Marshal Berg said, "Ms. Vanders, did Mrs. Gonzales give you the thumb drive?"

"Ah, ha! You see, Melody," Gregory said. "The FBI was listening to our conversations. Maria is dead, and you no longer need to keep her secret, so it's time to hand over that thumb drive."

"You're right," I said, as I dug in my purse and handed it to the Marshal Berg. "It contains an anecdote to a lethal bio weapon. Maria Gonzales wanted the Department of Health and Human Services to have it."

"We will let the FBI know all of this," Marshal Berg said.

"And now, it's time to go," Marshal Robinson said, "because we feel that the men who killed Maria Gonzales are out there looking for you."

As I walked outside to a waiting government car, I turned back toward Gregroy, "Don't forget the bank deposit, my deposit first!"

He patted his shirt pocket. "I won't."

I also noticed Marshal Robinson taping a large sign on my office door, OUT OF BUSINESS.

"I guess I really am moving now."

"Yes, Melody, that's the plan," Marshal Berg said, as she sat next to me in the back seat of the government car. "Now I need you to remove all forms of identification from your purse, driver's license, library, medical and grocery cards, and phone, and place them in this plastic bag."

"What will you do with them?"

"Shred them."

"And my laptop?"

"Marshall Robinson has it."

We drove away.

"Where are we going?" I asked.

"Just up the highway to the municipal airport. We have a small jet waiting for us on the tarmac, and the FBI will be there to see us off. Now, don't worry. Your go-bag is on board." Marshal Berg handed me a large manila envelope. "When we land at your new destination, I'll help you get a driver's license, but for now, take a look at your new passport and other forms of identification."

"But I never applied for a passport!"

"That doesn't matter. You have one now."

Being quite curious, I reached into the large envelope and retrieved my first and only passport. The photo was quite complimentary. My current real estate photo was enhanced with a larger smile and new clothing, but my address was shocking. "New York! It says my name is Melody Moore, and that I live in New York. Why not Hawaii or Florida?"

Marshal Bill Robinson said, "Your new home is in Youngstown. It's a small town near Buffalo."

"Oh, no, not Buffalo!" I whimpered.

Chapter 12
Youngstown, New York

When I landed at the Buffalo Airport, I was escorted to a waiting car. After the flight, I was on a first name basis with Marshals Maggie and Bill. I wore a blanket from the aircraft for extra warmth because the beautiful sixty-degree weather that I had left in Maryland, became a dreadful thirty-degree nightmare in Buffalo. Bill explained to me that they had an available residence for me in Youngstown, New York, which wasn't far from Buffalo. The current resident was a woman in her late sixties. Her name was Hilde Moore, and she would be my *Aunt Hilde*. With all the deception surrounding me, I didn't dare ask her real name. Nevertheless, we would be roommates, and no one knew how long I'd stay at that location.

Hilde and her husband Fred had moved to Youngstown about five years ago when they both retired from the U.S. Marshal's office, but moving to Youngstown never meant that their lives were no longer in danger.

"You see, Melody," Maggie said. "They both were placed in witness protection."

"Does that mean their identity has been changed?

"That's what witness protection means," she said.

"I think this loss of identity is dreadful."

"Melody, you have a choice: die, or change your identity."

"But leaving your friends and family behind is life-changing."

"Actually, Fred rather enjoyed his new small-town life, Hilde, too, until her husband succumbed to a heart attack less than a month ago."

"Do their neighbors know about their witness protection?

"No, and that information must never be disclosed," Maggie said. "Disclosing anything about this couple will put all of your lives in danger."

"What if anyone asks me about my so-called late uncle's past or his employment?"

"Your answer should always be short and simple, I don't recall ever meeting him. I was only a toddler when my mother and father visited Uncle Fred and Aunt Hilde."

Hilde was a great gal, friendly and cheerful. She even helped me write my obituary for an Eastern Shore newspaper. Apparently, Melody Vanders died in Baltimore, a car crash and in lieu of flowers, mourners were to send money to the local humane society or the fire company. My memorial stone would be placed in the cemetery next to my mother and father. Hilde made me sound like I was a successful Realtor and a model citizen with lots of admirers, but the real purpose of the obit was to explain to the Real Estate Board why I was no longer a member and no longer in business. A government attorney would handle my estate, which included the sale of my house, chattels, stocks, and money that I had in the bank. I later found out that Gregory did make my deposit and that both he and Earl were able to cash their checks. I was glad for that, and I'm sure they will continue cooking breakfast for Gladys if they were permitted to use her kitchen.

When I packed my go-bag, I didn't expect that I needed to dress so warmly, and with so few clothes, shopping in Buffalo was the first order of business. A debit card with a five-thousand-dollar limit was given to me to take care of my immediate needs until my own assets could be laundered and transferred to my account. But first, Aunt Hilde needed to give me an orientation on the do's and don'ts.

She instructed me to stay near the house for the next few weeks and not to venture out beyond our block. She wanted me to study my new personal history, and to know it so well that it rolled off my tongue. Most of all, she warned me to never-ever be in the public eye. Don't allow my picture to appear on social media, and have no interviews on TV, radio, podcasts, or journals. If I had to be moved suddenly, I would be given an appropriate cover story.

Chapter 13
Rescuing Gladys

By mid-December I realized that Youngstown, New York, can be spelled with four letters: C-O-L-D. It would be months before the temperature would warm to my liking. Aunt Hilde had received word from a source about Gregory, Earl, and Gladys. She explained that the news was old because it could never go directly to me, but rather it had to be laundered through other parties for my protection.

"Melody, I've heard from our contacts. There is some good news and some bad news. The morning after you left, Earl and Gregory went over to Gladys's house to prepare breakfast. When she didn't answer the door, they went inside."

"Did they break in?"

"No, apparently the door wasn't locked, but several lights were on in the house. That's why Earl and Gregory thought something was terribly wrong. They went inside and found Gladys locked in the hall closet and lying on the floor wrapped in a couple of winter coats."

"Is she okay?"

"She's fine, but the whole incident caused Gregory to contact the FBI immediately. He also called Gladys's daughter, who lives in Wisconsin. Rest assured, today Gladys is safe and living in a senior apartment near her daughter."

"Why was Gladys in the closet?"

"She told the FBI that she saw two men snooping around your house. She screamed at one of the intruders from her front porch and told him to go away."

"Oh, that's Gladys. She always had a brave streak in her."

"Her actions backfired because that man hopped up on her porch, and when he did, she noticed that he had a picture of you in his hand, your realtor photo."

"Of course, my photo was readily available online until I died."

"Gladys turned to go back into her house, and was then pushed inside. Rather than disclose that you were dead, she confessed that you had been picked up by the Feds. Of course, she wouldn't know where you are today, but that didn't stop the one man from threatening her."

"That's awful! What about the other man? Was Gladys physically abused?"

"Slightly, but I'm sure sleeping in close quarters for that long was miserable for her. Later, Gladys was able to recall the name of the man who locked her in the closet when the two men were talking."

"And now the U.S. Marshals have a new concern. Because Gladys had disclosed that you weren't dead, we must be more attentive to your safety."

"Does that mean I'll have to move again?"

"No, because Gladys doesn't know your new address. In addition, our office is having regrets that they didn't change your first name."

"But, keeping my first name makes it easy for me to keep my new identity."

"And easier for the bad guys to find you. Melody, your safety is no longer just about pharmaceutical formulas. It's about you being the only person who can positively identify the kidnappers and likely murderers of Dr. Morozov. We suspect they are the same ones who bullied Gladys and killed Maria and the people at the D.C. safehouse."

"What should I do?" I began to worry.

"Do as I had previously instructed, stay out of the public eye. Don't let anyone take your photo who would use it on social media or in the newspapers."

Chapter 14
Meeting the Neighbors

"Folks, there's no doubt about it, we will have a white Christmas!" the clock radio next to my ear spontaneously blared. "Nearly two feet of snow fell last night in Niagara Falls, and it looks like we could get a few more inches before this storm is over."

I sat up in bed and looked out the window. On the morning before Christmas, a heavy white blanket of snow seemed to have appeared without warning. Yesterday there were only a few small patches of ice on the ground, and now I was snow bound. The drifting snow had covered our front steps and had piled up several feet against the garage door. Aunt Hilde said we would be attending tonight's Christmas Eve church service with the Stevensons, but in order to do that, the neighborhood sidewalks needed to be cleared or we would be walking three blocks in the deep snow.

Youngstown, a quaint touristy village at the confluence of the Niagara River and Lake Ontario and is not far from the Falls. Because of its proximity to the Great Lakes, it was also subject to prodigious lake effect snows.

I pulled the blankets over my shoulders and sulked because I had no friends, and I couldn't stop thinking about my ruined real estate business that was just starting to show great promise. No doubt about it, I was quite sad. But my mother always said that if you're going to have a pity party, don't invite any guests, so I put on my happy face to meet the morning.

A big snow removal job required strategy, so I dressed warmly and walked out to the attached garage in search of equipment. Hanging on the wall was a snow shovel, so all that was left for me to do was to eat breakfast and discuss the job with Aunt Hilde. But before all of that, I knew the job also required a pot of coffee, a large pot. Aunt Hilde had prepared a lovely light breakfast of fruit and muffins from the local bakery.

Hilde poured a cup for me. "Sugar, cream?"

"Yes, please."

"Melody, my husband Fred recently died of a heart attack, and I'm sure the neighbors will be curious. But for your sake, tell any interested neighbor that you only met him when you were very young and have no memory of him. You can say, according to family members, your Uncle Fred was a kind and gentle man."

"I'm sure he was. It's clear to me that the man you would marry must have been a true gentleman."

"He was, Melody. We were both placed in witness protection, and for your safety I cannot disclose to you the circumstances that put me in this situation, but I know how you must be worried about your future. I certainly was at first. Now, enough of that talk. I need you to clear the snow off the front porch. Would you do that for me?

"Of course."

"One of the neighbors will finish clearing our sidewalks with a snowblower."

"Aunt Hilde, there is no way I can clear snow in my stiletto boots."

Aunt Hilde suggested that I look in the laundry room, where her husband's insulated gloves, heavy red plaid jacket, and a coif-crushing hat with oversized ear tabs were in the closet.

"Ah," I answered. "That's much better."

I was now dressed for the weather, even though Fred's boots were several sizes too big. I entered the garage, grabbed the snow shovel. I began shoveling the front porch, but the snow began falling at a faster rate, as if there were gigantic flour sifters shaking in the sky. I managed to clear the front steps, but before I finished, I heard a loud noise. *Burrum!* The sound waves roared like a jumbo jet at takeoff. So invasive was the noise that it knocked me off the porch steps and into a waist-high drift. Immediately the next-door neighbor turned off his snow blower and pulled me out of the drift. "Hello, I'm your neighbor Arthur Stevenson. Please allow me to finish this snow clearing for you."

It seemed as if he had everything under control, so after I thanked him several times and started to go back inside, I heard his voice.

"Hey, where are you going?" Mr. Stevenson asked.

"Inside," I said. "It's cold out here."

"But I'm gonna need some guidance with your aunt's narrow walkway up to her house. You certainly don't want me to damage her shrubbery with my shovel."

"No, sir. I wouldn't want that. My Aunt Hilde was kind enough to let me stay here, so the least I can do is protect her bushes."

"Now, that's the spirit, and I'm sure you are a great comfort to your aunt since her husband died. Where are you from?"

"Virginia." I was so proud of myself for remembering that bit of information. It was the first time my new identity was challenged.

"I bet there's not a lot of snow there, eh?"

"Actually, we do get quite a bit, but I don't think we've ever seen this much at one time."

"Well then, let me teach you a little trick, and I won't allow you to lift any of this heavy snow. Use your shovel and go straight down along the edges of the walkway up to the house to mark its location, and when I fire up the engine again, I'll clear it for you."

"Okay. I think I can handle that job." As I began marking the edges, Mr. Stevenson gave me a certain look of concern.

"Say, are you and your Aunt Hilde alone for Christmas Dinner? If so, my wife, Jane, and I would be happy to set two more plates at the table? Your Uncle Fred and Aunt Hilde always joined us for the Christmas candlelight service at the church. But this year, please join us for Christmas dinner, too."

"Thank you! That's so thoughtful. I'll mention it to Aunt Hilde, and I'm sure she'll be pleased to hear of your kind invitation."

"If you decide to come for dinner, please, come early for some hot apple cider, and we'll eat around four."

My job was cut short when Aunt Hilde called me into the house. I was glad for an excuse to thaw out because Mr. Stevenson was determined to keep me working outside until the last bit of hardscape was exposed.

"Mr. Stevenson is very kind, Aunt Hilde. I was helping him clear your walkways when he invited us to Christmas Dinner."

Aunt Hilde seems quite pleased. "I must call Mrs. Stevenson to confirm. Surely, she'll want me to go early and help her prepare the meal. You may be interested to know that the Stevensons have a son Chad about your age."

"Oh please, Aunt Hilde, I hope you're not scheming with your neighbors to set the two of us up."

"I wouldn't worry. Chad lives in Buffalo, and with so much snow, he may not make it home for Christmas."

Even with Fred's heavy gloves, my hands were still numb from the icy temperature and my nose was cherry red. As the morning wore on, all I could think about was a hot bath. I looked out the window. The weather was not letting up, and I could barely see the bushes along Hilde's walkway.

Some of the neighbors had returned outside to clear their driveways again. Hilde's front porch was covered with new snow, and it was evident that I would need to wear Uncle Fred's heavy boots in order to walk next door. No telling how deep the snow would be when it's time to walk home. Oh well, I thought. It was better to look like a lumberjack than to freeze my feet in sexy high heels.

I spent the next several minutes in the bathroom fixing my hair and putting on makeup. The polished southern belle in me wanted to wear a dress for dinner, but the weather made that choice impossible. So, I opted for my heaviest pants and a bulky seasonal sweater that Aunt Hilde loaned me, a loud, red-knit pullover. The Christmas tree on the front and back made it more fun than flattering.

It was nearing the hour that I was to be at the Stevensons' for dinner. I laced up Uncle Fred's boots and put on his fleece-lined cap over my fresh hairdo. His large, heavy jacket fastened easily over my bulky sweater, and before I put on his thick insulated gloves, I wrapped a long, knit scarf around my neck and face several times. I caught sight of myself in the mirror by the front door. I looked like the Michelin tire man on steroids. My eyes were my only exposed feature, making my shoulder purse the only evidence of femininity, but I was ready for dinner.

I opened the front door, and to my surprise, standing in front of me with a snow shovel in his hand was a tall, handsome guy who was about to ring the doorbell. He appeared to be at least six two or three with the most beautiful deep blue eyes. He was so good-looking that I gasped.

"Hi," he said. "I'm Chad Stevenson, and you must be Melody."

"Yes," I said with a muffled voice under multiple layers of wool scarf.

"I've come to help you walk next door. Your Aunt Hilde said that you may not be used to walking in so much snow and ice. In fact, I barely made it home driving from Buffalo."

I was utterly amazed that someone could be as tall and good-looking as Chad. I didn't want to stare at him, but I couldn't help myself. I think it was his big, beautiful blue eyes.

"Is something wrong?"

"No, no, not at all." Actually, everything was wrong. I should have paid more attention to Aunt Hilde's subtle suggestion about Chad. My outfit was all wrong for making a good impression. Uncle Fred's outerwear made me look like I had been shopping at the Goodwill.

Chad took my hand, though he couldn't possibly know how much it really meant to me through all the glove insulation.

"Hold onto the handrail. I shoveled the steps, but the leftover ice can be dangerous."

"Yes, of course." At this moment I wished that Aunt Hilde's porch had more than three steps. How could I possibly care about the dangerous ice while Chad was holding on to me?

"There, that wasn't so hard, was it?"

"No, not at all. It helped that you could steady my balance." What a big lie that was. Uncle Fred's boots were so big and heavy and wide that hurricane force winds would have left me standing.

Chad's mother June met us at the door as did a small boy who was hiding behind her legs. "Merry Christmas, Melody."

"Hi, Mrs. Stevenson! I can't thank you enough for inviting me to dinner.

"It's our pleasure." She gave me a welcoming hug.

"And who's the cute little fella with you?" I asked.

"This is our only grandson, Georgie." Mrs. Stevenson pointed to a large plastic bin next to the front door. "The two of you can leave your boots and wet clothes in this container, and please use our hall closet for your dry clothes."

"Thank you, Mrs. Stevenson." My growling stomach was glad that I'd soon be sitting down for dinner. I removed my coat, hat, scarf, and gloves and placed them in the appropriate places.

"Oh, Melody, what a beautiful sweater. I love Christmas clothes!"

"It's Aunt Hilde's, but it does seem perfect for the occasion."

"Ha, ha, ha!" Little Georgie laughed. "Your hair looks funny!"

Even Chad was smiling at me.

"Georgie, where are your manners?" June scolded, and then she turned to me with a sweet smile. "Melody, the powder room is that first door on your left down the hall, in case you'd like to use it."

June left the front hall while Chad and I removed our boots. We were both left with stocking feet. He continued to look at me with great intensity. *Hmm, maybe he thinks I'm attractive. That's hard to believe, because this behemoth sweater makes me look like the circus fat lady.*

I stepped into the powder room and closed the door. In the mirror I saw horror of all horrors. I instantly realized why Chad was staring at me, and why little Georgie was laughing. My hair was matted down so badly from Uncle Fred's cap that it was clumped to one side. There was a quiet knock on the door.

"Melody," Mrs. Stevenson voice was low.

"Yes?" I opened the door a crack.

"Take your time, and come join us in the family room when you're ready. We have a wonderful roaring fire in there."

After straightening my appearance, I wandered through the dining room toward the rear of the house. The holiday table was elegantly set with fine china and sparkling crystal. The beautiful red napkins were tied with green plaid ribbons, and a gold damask center runner was draped over the bright white linen tablecloth. While I searched for my place card, I could hear voices in the next room. I stood in the doorway and looked into the Stevensons' family room. The star atop their large, fresh tree almost touched the ceiling, and its brilliant-colored lights and numerous ornaments reminded me of home and how Mother always made sure we had a lovely tree as well.

The room was spacious and paneled with wide tongue-and-groove pine boards. There were animal trophies on the wall, a stuffed pheasant, and four bucks, all wearing red and white elf hats. Above the fireplace was a large framed photograph of Arthur Stevenson and his son when Chad was a young boy. I stifled a laugh. Both were holding fish. Chad's fish was almost half his height, whereas George's fish was about the size of his palm. Above the doorways and windows was a wide shelf that extended the entire perimeter of the room and was filled with baseball trophies. Anyone could see that baseball was Chad's longtime ambition. He must have lived and breathed the sport for most of his life.

"Come in, come in, please," Chad said as he stood near his parents. "Meet the rest of the family." He introduced me to his sister and her husband, and once again to little Georgie. Chad poured me a cup of hot apple cider and gave me his chair.

"Thank you, Chad. I can see by all these baseball trophies that you are quite an athlete."

"And he still is!" His father was quick to boast. "Chad is now a pitcher with the Buffalo Bisons. They know how to recognize talent."

I looked at Mr. Stevenson. "I love baseball. My father took me to several games when he was still well enough to go." I stood up and looked more closely at Chad's trophy case. "Chad, you have certainly amassed quite a collection and a few state records."

"Oh, that's nothing." Chad said. "They're mostly Little League and high school awards."

"And several Buffalo University awards, too." Mr. Stevenson was visibly proud of his son. "Chad was also president of the Christian Men's Athletic Association. That's what this award is all about."

Upon closer inspection, I could see that Chad's state records were true marks of excellence. "Wow, Chad, this is incredible--a state record! I have a state record, but it's nothing like this."

"Oh, really?" June was all ears.

"Yes, I flunked my driving road test eight times. It, too, was a state record, but I passed on my ninth try."

Mr. Stevenson laughed out loud. "Well, I'm glad you told me because I was going to loan you my truck."

"Thank you, but I couldn't drive in this much snow."

"Well, then tomorrow, Chad, why don't you take Melody around town? And while you're out, show her some of the local historical sights."

"I'd be happy to do that," Chad said.

June smiled. "Good, then that's settled. Your Aunt Hilde is a good friend of ours, and we want you to feel right at home here in Youngstown."

I looked at Chad and noticed a twinkle in his eyes. He put his hand on my shoulder. "Then I'll pick you up tomorrow around ten?"

"Ten will be fine," I said.

"Chad is a very good tour guide," Mrs. Stevenson said. "He's up on our local history. I just know you'll have a fun time."

"Melody, our family has opened all of our presents, but we have one for Hilde."

Hilde took the present and smiled as she thanked Mrs. Stevenson.

"And this one's for you, Melody."

I was stunned. The Stevensons had been so kind that I wasn't prepared for this additional bit of hospitality. June pulled a gift bag from under the tree. I was so overwhelmed by their generosity. Inside the bag, and carefully wrapped with tissue, was a fashionable winter hat that was perfect for the current weather. I think June felt sorry for me because I was stuck with Uncle Fred's winter garments. Whether the hat was one from her closet or regifted, it was a lovely gesture and certainly something I needed. "Thank you, everyone. You have really made me feel very special this Christmas."

"You're certainly welcome," June replied for everyone. "Now, while the turkey is resting and before we sit down for dinner, I think we should sing a few carols. Chad, do you mind playing your guitar?"

Chad lifted his guitar from a hook on the wall and checked the tune. "What shall we sing first?

June chimed in, "Melody, as our guest, why don't you pick the first song. Hilde, you'll be second, and then we'll go around the room. After we've sung everyone's favorite carol, Mr. Stevenson will say grace."

Arthur Stevenson nodded, "My pleasure."

"And then can we eat, Grandma?"

"Yes, Georgie, that's when we'll go to the dining room for our Christmas dinner."

"Melody, what carol should I play first?" Chad said.

"How about Hark the Herald Angels Sing, Glory to Our Newborn King!"

As we began signing, Hilde's eye welled up. I put my arm around her. There was no doubt in anyone's mind that she missed her husband.

Chapter 15
Winter Fun with Chad

The following morning after breakfast, I felt much more relaxed when Chad stopped by Aunt Hilde's house. This time, when I met him at the front door, I was ready to be on a date with a great looking guy. The snow glistened in the clear sunlight, making it impossible to go outside without sunglasses. The temperature had also dropped a few more degrees, but the frigid air didn't hinder the neighborhood children from building snowmen in their front yards, nor did it keep the public works department from plowing the streets and sidewalks, which made it easy to walk outside and climb into Chad's SUV. But before he could close my door, a man shouted from across the street.

"Hey, Chad! Thanks again for visiting my grandson in the hospital.

I want you to know that little Frankie sleeps with that ball you autographed for him."

"Is he home now?" Chad asked.

"Yeah, just in time for Christmas."

"Give him my best, and I'll see if I can't get some tickets for his family."

"Hey, thanks, Chad."

"You're welcome." Chad got behind the wheel and smiled at me. "What do you think of all this snow?"

"How could I think of the snow when I'm so impressed by your kindness?"

"That's nice of you to say. You know, Melody, we don't normally get four feet all at one time. But then, we New Yorkers know how to manage it when it comes."

We drove toward the downtown district, past the old brick school house, which was now home to the town's library, municipal offices, and the police department. Then we continued on until we reached Main Street where we parked. Our first stop was to a local coffee shop. Chad thought it was best to plan our day over a cup of coffee.

"Hey, Angelo," Chad called out to the young man behind the counter. "This is Melody, she's new in town."

We sat down in front of the fireplace on a cozy overstuffed sofa and sipped our coffee.

We looked into each other's eyes and shared a slight giggle as if we both knew we'd like to share a kiss.

Just to change the subject, I asked Chad about his pitching career.

"There's not much to tell until this season is over. It's my rookie year with the Bisons. Before that I played at Buffalo University and in high school. I figured that some major league team would ask me to sign before I graduated from Buffalo, but they didn't. It worried me some until finally I was offered me a pitching contract with the Bisons."

"I'm excited for you. You've dedicated so many years to the sport, and you've been rewarded with a contract."

"Now that you know all about me, tell me what made you want to move in with your Aunt Hilde?"

I paused for a moment to recall my cover story. I had been warned me not to disclose much information about myself. "Let's just say that my real estate business didn't turn out as I expected, and I needed a change. Besides, after Uncle Fred died, I was glad that Aunt Hilde offered to take me in." Anxious to change the subject, I said, "Now that you've shown me this charming place, where's our next stop?"

"How about we start at Fort Niagara State Park? It's just down the street, and it's loaded with history and has a great hill for sledding. The place dates back to 1726, when the British were at war with the French, and during WWII it housed German and Austrian POWs, mostly the officers. We could walk, but I'd rather use up my extra energy sledding down the hill."

"Sledding?" I asked.

"Yep. That is, if you're up to it."

"Sure. I can't remember the last time I went sledding, but I do remember how fun it was."

"Then finish your coffee, and we'll go. My sled is behind the back seat."

We drove to the park and stopped by the river bank overlooking the mouth of the Niagara River where it flows out into Lake Ontario. Near the park's entrance sat a hill about three or four stories high, totally out of character with the rest of the terrain. After the war, most of the brick buildings that housed the POWs were torn down, and the remaining rubble that wasn't recycled became the "hill," which was later covered with dirt and seeded with grass.

"How do we reach the top?" I asked.

"You just climb. It helps you keep warm."

My legs were a little sore by the time we reached the top of the hill. "It looks much higher from up here," I said, as I started to feel dizzy, but I didn't want to let on to Chad that I was terrified of heights.

"Come on, it's our turn to get on the sled," he said.

Chad's arms gently circled my waist, and my heart fluttered as we sat down on the sled close to the edge of the hill. I positioned myself in the front, and Chad wrapped his legs around me so he could plant them firmly on the bow of the sled.

"Look over there, Melody, across Lake Ontario. Do you see that city skyline?"

"Yes, I do."

"That's Toronto."

And before I could get another look, Chad pushed off and down the hill we went. The speed was as fast as an amusement park ride. It felt as though I had left my stomach at the top of the hill as we reached the bottom. To stop our forward motion, we rolled off together, laughing as we tumbled over each other in the soft snow.

As we lay next to each other in the snow, Chad brushed the loose flakes off my face. "You're very lovely, Melody."

My heart stopped. I couldn't believe my ears. Chad is the kind of guy who only appears in my dreams, not in person, and he just said that I was pretty. "Thank you," I said with a gentle smile. "I'm having a great time, Chad."

"Would you like to go again?" he asked.

"I'll go as many times as my strength allows me to climb up to the top."

Slowly, we once again reached the top of the steep incline and waited our turn. This time I got a better look at Lake Ontario and at the Toronto skyline. I much preferred looking out across the lake than looking down and trembling.

We positioned ourselves for takeoff. I felt like a little kid as we flew down the side of the hill. At the bottom, Chad helped me to my feet and looked into my eyes with an inviting smile.

"Let's warm up in the park's museum, and then I'll take you to lunch. How does that sound?"

"It sounds wonderful."

The diner overlooked the Niagara River and the Youngstown Yacht Club below. The view was first class, and the menu was good hometown fare.

The moment that Chad and I entered the restaurant, Chad caught the attention of many local fans.

"Chad, how about a selfie of me, you and your girl?" One young man shouted.

"Not me," I insisted, "but you go ahead," which he did without me.

Chad and I were then ushered to a quiet table in the back of the restaurant that had the best view of the river. We took off our outerwear and sat down, but before opening the menu, Chad took my hand and said, "How would you like to go to church with me this Sunday?"

"I'd like that very much," His invitation caught me off-guard. Never before had a date asked me to church. It was a warm and pleasant surprise that meant more to me than a bouquet of flowers. It would also make my father smile because he always told me the best men are found in church.

Chad kissed my hand and stared into my eyes with a romantic twinkle. "I had a great time today."

"So did I, Chad."

"Then let's go again tomorrow! There are so many other places I want to show you. We'll have fun. I promise."

We decided to see the Falls, but it was more like experiencing its roar and terrifying power. I felt lightheaded as I held my stomach and peered over the edge. I was glad for the opportunity to see its magnificence, but I soon became dizzy and unstable. Seeing my uneasiness, Chad stepped closer to me. I could feel his warm breath as he whispered in my ear, "Come, Melody. Let's head back to the car."

When I arrived home, I invited Chad in for a cup of hot cocoa. "I believe Aunt Hilde is playing bridge across the street and will probably be home soon. You can hang your coat in the hall closet."

When Chad opened the closet, he saw a guitar, which he picked up and smiled. "I remember listening to your uncle playing songs on this thing. He had quite a repertoire."

"Would you like to play it?"

"Well, yes, I suppose so. I have a Willie Nelson song in mind. I'm a bit of a romantic, and when a song speaks to my traditional, old-fashioned heart, I want to sing it."

"In my book, traditional is a good thing, so let's hear your rendition of Willie's song."

Chad strummed the strings and then began to play and sing his song:

"Sometimes I wonder how I spend each lonely night dreaming of a song." (Now, this is where I add my own lyrics.) "My Melody (That's you.) haunts my reverie, and I'm once again with you, and each kiss and an inspiration."

"Chad! Those are very fine words."

"I'm glad you think so. I was afraid you'd think it's corny."

"Not at all! Do you have more to this song?"

"'Fraid not, but I'm working on it."

Over the next few weeks, the time that I shared with Chad filled a void in my life. We went to dinner on New Year's Eve and danced to all the slow songs. Being with him made me feel complete. I didn't look for this love, but rather his love found me.

On his last night before leaving for Florida, Chad and I lingered on Aunt Hilde's front porch. The wintery night air was crisp and the sky clear. Chad stood behind me with his warm chest pressed firmly against my back as he wrapped his arms around me with a gentle squeeze. We watched the full moon rise above the tall oak tree in the Stevenson's front yard as it peered through its highest boughs. Sadness fell over me as I realized Chad would be leaving for spring training in the morning.

"Melody."

"Yes, Chad."

He looked at me with great tenderness. "Melody, all my life I had this dream that I would play professional ball, and my dreams have come true. Tomorrow I'll join my fellow players, but now that I'm leaving, I never thought it would be so hard to say goodbye. I thank you for making my time here in Youngstown so special."

"I plan to watch you play every game in Buffalo. I'll get season tickets, so you'll see me sitting in the same place for every game, on the first base line a few rows above the dugout."

Chad smiled wide. "And I'll always look for you in that special place."

We kissed good night just inside Aunt Hilde's house. It was not a simple kiss. It was a kiss that spoke to our beating hearts, telling us that we should never be apart. He promised to call me regularly, which softened my sadness. I felt so connected to Chad, as if I had known him for years. I knew I would miss him, but he would return home before opening day in April.

Chapter 16
Goodbye, Dear Hilde

I'll never forget a certain middle of the night episode. It was a frightening moment for me when Hilde came to my room and woke me up from a deep sleep. "Get up, Melody." She shook me gently. "The U.S. Marshals are here."

Barely awake and with tousled hair and puffy eyes, I managed to crawl out of bed and slip on my robe. We walked into the living room, and I looked out my window where the blinking lights of an ambulance parked out front reflected against the white snow on the front lawn. Two men with a stretcher stepped up onto the porch, and as they entered the house, I recognized the men as U.S. Marshals whom I had met previously.

"My cover has been breached," Hilde said to me. "You and I will need to move to another residence."

"That's right," one of the Marshals said. "Both of you must vacate this house now. Hilde will leave on this stretcher, and you'll ride in the car parked in front of the ambulance."

"Do I have time to dress?"

"Yes, of course, but don't dally," the Marshal said, "and once we're a few miles away, I want you to call your neighbors next door and tell them that Hilde has had a serious stroke, and you will be going with her to the hospital. Do not disclose any additional information."

I watched as Hilde laid down on the stretcher. She took my hand and smiled. "Melody, you realize this is our last time together."

73

I nodded and kissed her cheek, knowing it was a final goodbye.

Hilde was strapped onto the gurney and a blanket covered all but her face. We gazed at one another with deep sadness.

Looking around the room, "What about our things?" I asked.

"A moving van will be he here sometime this week. They'll gather everything in this house and place it in our secure storage. You can retrieve your belongings from there."

"And Hilde? What should I say if anyone asks? The neighbors certainly will call me for an update on Hilde."

"You simply say that she passed away quietly. You're going to be given a new cellphone, a new identity, and a new residence. Within the week Hilde's stone will be placed next to her late husband's grave and her obit will show up online and in the local paper. In the meantime, we're taking you to the FBI field office in Buffalo. You'll stay out of sight until we can find other accommodations for you."

"Will this be my final move? If so, why Buffalo and not a nice condo in Florida?"

"Melody, there is something you must know, and I going to tell you this only so you will understand how devious and cruel your enemies can be. The toxicology report came back on Hilde's husband Fred. He didn't die of a natural heart attack, but one that was chemically induced. We believe it was a poison dart with a sting so slight; it probably felt like an insect bite. So, you see, we must make sure you are kept in the safest places possible and you may never take any chances that would expose your true identity."

"Believe me, I'll do whatever you ask to protect my life."

"Good, because we believe the bad guys will do whatever it takes to protect their reputation. Well, we don't need to dwell on the worst-case scenario."

74

I dressed quickly and watched as the Marshals wheeled Hilde out the door and into a waiting ambulance. It was time for us to leave.

My sleep deprived body shuffled down the hallway of the Buffalo FBI building. In a few short months my psyche had gone from an always in control to *que sera, sera*. My life was no longer mine because I was at the mercy of the government. This left me clueless as to what to expect next.

I was escorted to a conference room and took a seat at the large table that appeared to be standard government issue, very practical with no glitz. My mind briefly wandered as I continued to look around the room. *Perhaps I'm a suspect rather than the victim. Maybe these G-men are planning to make me the fall-gal for the murders.* But it wasn't the case, just my wee hours of the night imagination.

I now realized that the Feds had been watching me, even while I was seeing Chad. Their concern was valid. Apparently, I had been tailed by various FBI individuals, both male and female. But in the meantime, Agent Spence laid out the next plan.

To protect me as an important federal witness, the government would provide me with a house in Buffalo, which they claimed would be safe, although the house wouldn't be ready for a few weeks because stealthy background checks on all the neighbors had to be done. The only positive thing about Buffalo was that I'd be close to Chad once the season began.

Agent Spence wore a mean poker face and a flat top head of hair. His personality was cold and professional, and his steely blue eyes seemed to match his demeanor. There was no room for levity with this fed. He was all business, the government's business. But not wanting to bite the hand that was providing me a safety near Chad, I put on my best face and listened. Spence laid before me six photographs and asked if I recognized any of the men who attacked Ivan Morozov. One photo matched perfectly. He was a tall, husky man with dark hair and furry eyebrows, and I'll never forget his large jawline.

"Melody, now that we've made a positive identification on one of the suspects, we still need to find his partner. We have no idea where they currently are, but we're sure they will surface soon. This means your life continues to be in danger, and Marshal Berg will be assigned to keep you safe, but you must stay out of the spotlight. After you move into your new home, you can live a normal life as long as you follow certain rules. If you ever feel like your life is in danger, you are to call this number, which has been programmed into your new cellphone, but I want you to memorize the number as well. When you call it, the operator will immediately connect you to me, Agent Spence. Any questions?"

"Yes, there were two men who abducted Dr. Morozov. Will you be able to find the other man?"

"We'll do our best. Gladys Cutler gave us a description the man you just identified. It means that we're getting close. These bad guys can only be charged with murder if you can identify them in court, and believe me, these evil-doers are looking under every rock to find you. Their bosses have big budgets, sophisticated technology, and long tentacles that will make it possible to find you."

"Oh, Maggie, I'm frightened."

"In your situation, fear is healthy and reasonable." Maggie slid a small box in front of me. "Here's your new cellphone. You will receive no phone bills as those expenses will be paid by our department. Tomorrow, your current phone will stop working. Do not make any calls on your old phone, but answer any calls from the next-door neighbor. Remember, Hilde is dead. We expect they will call you about Aunt Hilde within the next twenty-four hours."

"Of course."

"Now, inside this envelope is your new identity. Start using your new name, Jill Malone.

"Jill Malone? Why can't it be Melody Malone. It has a nice ring to it?"

"It's Jill," Maggie replied with stern authority, and you must start using it immediately."

"No! I'm not changing my first name, and that's final. Tell your superiors, I'm Melody Malone and not Jill.

"Okay, okay, I'll let them know. They won't be happy, but I believe I can convince them it's for the best."

After my orientation, I walked out with Maggie to her car, located under the building. She opened the trunk and put her suitcase next to puny my go-bag.

"Don't worry, we'll get your clothes out of storage tomorrow. In the meantime, we have two options, with or without an indoor pool." Maggie paused very briefly. "We'll take the hotel with the pool. Come on, let's go. The sun is rising."

As the garage door opened, the cold wind whipped through the parking garage, giving my face a painful burning sensation. Buffalo in the wintertime couldn't possibly be colder than the North Pole, but I began to wonder. We hopped in her car and headed for the hotel.

Over the next few days, Maggie and I became close friends, but in a most professional way. It was like having an older sister, although she never let her guard down to protect me. We both were unhappy about the situation. She missed her husband at night, and I missed having a place to call home. We made the most of it by swimming in the hotel's indoor pool, getting manicures at the hotel salon, and by watching endless hours of home and garden shows on the television. During the day, I'd hang out with her partner Bill, mostly at bowling alleys. Although I enjoyed the game, he was a bowling bully, but Bill was a good sport by not insisting we bowl every day. We also played endless games of cribbage and scrabble, and many times we simply felt like reading books or the daily papers. He noticed that I was always wanted the sports pages.

"Do you like baseball?" Bill asked.

"As a matter of fact, I do. I was looking at the Buffalo Bisons' schedule. It was just released; I can't wait for opening day. I want to buy season tickets, so I can have a regular seat along the first base line."

"The stadium seating is in today's paper. Mark which seat you want, and I'll make the purchase for you."

"Thank you, Bill. That's so nice of you."

"It's no problem. I love baseball, and I'll always be seated next to you."

The days turned into weeks, and one morning after breakfast Maggie escorted me down to the hotel lobby where I always met Bill. I knew that something was up from the happy tone of his voice.

"You gals will have to go back to your room and pack your things. The new safe house is ready. You can move into your home today. Here are the keys. It's a small bungalow in a well-established area of Niagara Falls."

"Today?" Maggie was skeptical. "Melody is moving today?"

"Yep. I got the call early this morning, and I knew both of you would be thrilled."

"You can say that again," Maggie declared. "Being cooped up in a Buffalo hotel room in the middle of winter is not an ideal situation."

"Your new place is furnished with items from our warehouse. You'll probably recognize a few pieces from Hilde's house, but don't get too comfortable. Moving you to this location, only makes it more difficult for the bad guys to find you, and there's aways a possibility that you'll be moving again." Bill said.

"Then can my next move be somewhere in Hawaii?"

"Not when the trial will be held in Baltimore," Maggie said. "The Attorney General will want to keep you in the Northeast area, and until both suspects are captured, you may have to move again."

Bill said, "For now, we believe this Niagara Falls bungalow offers good security, but that could change."

Chapter 17
Chad Gets a Roommate

"Strike three, and oh what a game!" The stadium announcer's enthusiasm bellowed out over the P.A. "Chad Stevenson has just won another one for the season."

As Chad and his teammates walked off the field, Keith, the pudgy assistant manager, said, "Good game, Chad, good game." Keith's talents were his encyclopedic knowledge of baseball stats and his jolly attitude. "I love the way you caught the last batter looking, a curve ball right on the corner."

"Thanks," Chad said.

In the locker room, Keith pointed to the inside of Chad's locker. "Where's your girl?"

"Yeah, Melody. I don't have her picture, but if I did it would be right here."

Keith gave Chad a fraternal slap on the back. "Everything seems to be happening for you, pal. You're going places. I can tell."

"Yeah, like back to Buffalo tomorrow."

"And speaking of Buffalo, I gotta roommate for you, a pitcher. I gave him your cell number and apartment address."

Chad looked around the locker room. "Oh, yeah? And which one of these guys is the one?"

"He's not here. He's not supposed to leave New York."

"Why? Who is this guy?"

"His name is Denton."

"Denton? As in Denton, the felon, Fenton?" Chad said.

"Yeah, he's the one, and from what I've heard, the front office got him real cheap."

Chad looked at Keith with disbelief. "But I thought he was in prison."

"He was. He's getting out early on good behavior and all of that stuff."

"So, you didn't just get him from the Yankee's pen, but from the State pen."

"Ha, that's a good one, Chad!" Keith laughed so hard through his gnarled teeth that his glasses slipped off his nose. "The club bought his contract just after the judge put him on home detention with the stipulation that he can't leave the state of New York. Of course, that means we can only use him at home games and in Syracuse and Rochester. But we still think we got a great deal."

"Sounds to me like the Yankees had enough of his drug addiction."

"Hey, the guy's clean now, and he's agreed to regular drug tests. There's nothing to worry about."

"How about his stamina?"

"Ah, Chad, don't you worry about Denton. He's been working out a lot. In fact, last summer while pitching on a prison team, he had five no-hitters."

"Great," Chad rolled his eyes. "So, I'm gonna have a felon ace for a roommate."

"Hey, we have to put him with someone. Besides, you're the team's straightest shooter."

"Gee thanks. This is my reward for staying out of trouble?"

"Don't let it get to you. Denton's a funny guy and a great knuckleballer. I just know the two of you will get along just fine."

"Just fine?" Chad scowled.

"Don't feel so sour about all of this. Here, let me make it up to you." Keith reached into his pocket and pulled out a piece of paper. "Have a couple of half-off coupons at KFC. Fried chicken always makes me feel better."

Chad was proud to show off his new place to his parents. He unlocked the door to his furnished Buffalo apartment. It was a modern two-bedroom, one-bath place that was located just off of the Scajaquada Expressway, a ten-minute drive from the ballpark, depending on traffic.

"Well, Mom, what do you think?" Chad said as he set two sacks of groceries on the kitchen counter.

His father looked around the room. "It's quite functional, I would say. And the fact that it's on the second floor is good."

"Now, Arthur," Chad's mother interrupted, "It's an apartment. What did you expect? I say it sure beats that college place that he shared with three other guys."

"You're right, Jane, and it's close to the ballpark."

"Have you heard from Melody?" Jane asked.

"Not since her Aunt Hilde died. I had Melody's phone number, but it's no longer in service."

"That's a shame," Jane said. "We liked her very much. What do you feel like eating?"

"How about just a sandwich? I don't want you to go to so much trouble, Mom. I'd rather visit with you and Dad. With my schedule, I may not get to see you for a while."

The Stevensons' conversation was abruptly interrupted by a loud knock at the door.

"Excuse me." Chad crossed the room and opened the front door, only to see a man nearly filling the doorway. You must be Denton."

"Yep, I sure am." Denton's hair, which was more brown than blond, looked as if it had never been combed, only washed, and his mischievous smile and twinkling brown eyes indicated that the Bisons were in for one uniquely challenging season. Denton extended a hand indicating that he would allow the fine gentleman accompanying him into the house first.

"Well, Denton," Chad shook his hand. I guess this is your place, too."

"You guessed right, Chadster. Fat-boy Keith said we'd be roommates, so I hope you don't my mind my unannounced intrusion."

Mr. and Mrs. Stevenson taken aback by Denton's rude comments about Keith.

"Denton, I want you to meet my mom and dad, Arthur and Jane Stevenson."

Denton tipped his ball cap at Chad's parents. "And this guy here is Officer Scott, that's his last name as you can see by the shiny brass nameplate pinned to his shirt."

"Maybe I should make more sandwiches," Jane suggested.

"Great idea. Me and Scottie are hungry."

"Please, don't make one for me," Officer Scott said. "I'll be leaving shortly."

Denton immediately made himself at home by removing his black leather jacket and a long white scarf and tossing them on the coffee table. His snug-fitting, long-sleeved shirt showed off his broad muscular upper body, which towered over the sturdy but lithe officer.

Denton put his hand on Scott's shoulder, which the officer abruptly removed.

"Scottie, allow me to introduce my roommate Chad Stevenson." Denton smiled broadly as if Scottie was his new best friend.

"How do you do?" The officer nodded. "And it's Officer Scott. I shouldn't be long, just long enough to set up this monitoring device."

Chad looked at his parents who were surprised by Denton's entrance. "Denton is one of our pitchers for Buffalo."

Jane was speechless and wide-eyed and Arthur, who was equally flabbergasted, managed to choke out a few words. "But, Denton, I thought you were in pris…."

"Prison? That's right, Pop. I got out today, and now I'm on home detention, which means I can get back to my pitching. Say, there, Chadster! Put 'er there." Denton firmly shook Chad's hand. "How was spring training?"

"Warmer than Buffalo," Chad answered.

"Sorry I missed the party, but Judge Burton wouldn't let me leave New York."

Officer Scott interrupted. "Now, Denton, if you will take a seat, it won't take long to calibrate the device to this address."

"That's right," Denton laughed. "Beam me up, Scottie. Energize! Energize!"

The officer knelt down to put the bracelet around Denton's right ankle.

"Hey, Scottie, whatcha doing there? I'm a right-handed pitcher. Left leg, left leg! Please! I don't want this thing messing with my E.R.A."

"Okay, I gotcha. Then hold up your left pant leg." He fastened the monitor to Denton's left ankle and then stood up. "Let me explain this device to you, and then I'll be on my way."

"Yeah, Scottie, give it to me straight."

Officer Scott read from a paper attached to his clipboard. "This is an electronic monitoring device, also known as the EMD. It uses a combination of cellular technology and global positioning systems, also known as GPS. What this device tracks your whereabouts in real time. You can be in a building, on a train, or a bus and it knows where you are. Any law enforcement officer can visit a secured website to see your exact location at any given time. You are to remain in this apartment at all times. You are only permitted to leave when on work release…"

Denton smiled, as if he were telling a joke. "Work release, that means when I'm pitching for the team."

Officer Scott continued, "…and only when you are under the direct supervision of your employer. Is that clear?"

"Absolutely clear, Scottie."

"Good," Officer Scott said, "so let me continue to read this statement. You are not permitted to leave the State of New York. If you do, the nearest law enforcement authorities will be notified immediately. You are not permitted to remove this device from your body. If you do, a signal will automatically alert our monitoring system, and law enforcement officers will be immediately notified. If this should occur, your probation will be revoked."

"That means I go back to the big house." Denton said.

"Precisely," Officer Scott said, and then he continued. "Now, do you have any questions?"

"No, sir." Denton smiled and winked at Jane.

"Then sign right here." Officer Scott handed Denton a pen.

"Autographs, I love giving autographs." Denton signed his name and took his copy.

"Now, if you'll excuse me," Officer Scott said, "I must be going."

Ah really, Scottie?" And I was just beginning to like you," Denton followed him to the door.

"Hold it there, Denton!" Officer Scott pointed downward at the threshold. "Do you see this?"

"Yes, sir!" Denton answered.

"If you cross this threshold to leave, it will set off an alarm on my phone. Understand?"

"Ah, bummer, that means I won't be able to take out the trash."

"Exactly," Officer Scott replied as he turned to leave. "Good night, all."

Denton closed the door behind the officer, and looked at Chad. Hey, I'm sorry man, but you heard Scottie. You're stuck with me in this apartment, and I'm not supposed to take out the trash." Denton looked around the room at everyone. "Oh, well, let's not have sad faces." Denton walked over to the refrigerator and opened the door. "Do you have anything to drink? Hey, Labatts Blue, my favorite!" He took one out, unscrewed the cap, and took a big swig. "Thanks, Chad!" He paused a moment. "Hey, why are we all standing around? Come on, have a seat. Make yourselves at home," he said, chuckling as he plopped down on the sofa.

Arthur took a comfortable seat in the living room. "So, Denton, how long must you wear this device of yours?"

"Ah, just a few months, Pop, and then I'll be able to play outta state." Denton lifted his pant leg to get a closer look at his EMD. "Shh...sugar! Oops, pardon me ma'am, almost said a bad word. I don't like to cuss around women, but daggone! This thing is covering up my favorite tattoo."

"And what's so special about your... ah... tattoo?" Jane asked.

"I got it just after I struck out the side in nine pitches. It was against Baltimore, and the first time I had ever done it. Of course, I haven't done that since, so you can see why this means so much to me. Too bad I can't show it to you, but if you look really close, you can see part of it."

"No thank you," Jane replied. "Perhaps I'll see it after your ankle bracelet is removed. Besides, Arthur and I must be going. Shouldn't we, darling?"

"Yes," Arthur agreed as he stood up. "It was good to meet you, Denton. I'm sure we'll be seeing more of you during the season."

"I'm sure." Denton belched in a deep, satisfying manner. "Oops, pardon me. I love this Blue, but it affects me some."

"Come on, dear, it's getting late," Jane beckoned her husband as she walked over to the front door. "Chad, please call us, and don't be a stranger."

"Don't worry, Mom." He kissed her cheek.

"And let us know when you're scheduled to pitch," Arthur added as he shook his son's hand.

The Stevensons left, and Chad closed the door behind them. He turned around and leaned against the door. There was a moment of silence before he took a deep breath and looked sternly at Denton. "The larger bedroom is mine."

Denton lifted his bottle in a salute. "I was gonna suggest that."

Chad picked up his suitcase and started for the back bedroom.

"Hey, Chadster, you don't have to go to bed so soon, do you? Stick around and have a beer on me."

"Nah, you go ahead. I've got to make a couple of calls."

Chapter 18
The First Home Games

I finally got to move into my new place in Niagara Falls. Although I owned none of the household items, not even a dish towel, my bungalow was beginning to feel like home. I couldn't wait to show it to Chad, though I hadn't told Agents Maggie or Spence that I wanted to see him.

Chad, Chad, Chad. The mere thought of him melted my heart. Every moment of every day I had some vision of me with him, like sailing on Lake Ontario, dancing to slow music, or simply looking into his eyes. I missed him terribly, and then one evening around eight I heard on the television that he was back in Buffalo.

The Buffalo Bison's first home game was Thursday and Saturday Chad was scheduled to pitch. I decided to call Chad. Although he didn't have my new number, I certainly had his. Maggie and Spence had warned me not to disclose my situation to him, at least not yet. It was for his protection as well as mine, but I couldn't bear the thought of not seeing Chad, so I called him.

"When will I get to see you?" he asked. "Tonight?"

"Tonight! Yes, that would be great." My heart rate increased just thinking about reuniting with Chad. Deep inside I thought that I should use some measure of restraint, but my hasty answer failed to consider my instincts. I wanted to see him, and that was that.

It's been too long since Chad held me in his arms. It's been too long since we kissed, and the only chance we'll have to be together is between games when he's in town. I gave Chad my address and turned on my porch light.

"And I'll be right there," he said.

I was overwhelmed with joy, but I knew I must call Maggie and let her know.

"Maggie, Chad is coming over. That's okay, isn't it?"

"No," she replied with a stern voice. "Bill and I haven't developed a plan for you to see Chad, and this isn't it. But just for tonight, I'll let it slide, even though you are putting his life in danger." Maggie's voice was stern. "Until we know where all the assassins are located, you cannot be seen with Chad, so make your meeting tonight brief, very brief for his sake."

"I will. Thank you, Maggie."

"You're welcome, but in the future, you must first ask us to set up a meeting."

"I will, and I promise to make tonight's visit here brief."

"Have a nice evening. I know that you're anxious to see Chad."

Chapter 19
Three is a crowd

Chad was thrilled to see Melody and whistled all the way home. When he pulled into the parking lot of his apartment complex, he discovered that someone had taken his spot. His car was subject to towing if he parked in the wrong place, so Chad drove onto the street and began looking for a place to park. It wasn't easy, but he managed to find a place about a block away and walked back to his apartment. His high spirits after having a fun evening out, kept him from being too annoyed by the inconvenience.

When he opened the door to his apartment, Chad saw Denton grabbing two beers from the refrigerator.

"Hey, Denton, haven't you had enough of my beer?"

After a long and satisfying belch, Denton looked at the two bottles in his hands and said, "not really." He then chuckled and said, "Oops, these are the last ones."

"I didn't buy the beer for you."

"Here." Denton handed Chad a beer. "Drink this one, and I can split this other."

"Split it with whom?"

"Jasmine." Chad put the other beer back into the refrigerator.

"Jasmine? Who in the world is Jasmine?"

"My girl... uh, sort of. She's been sending me these letters, and I've been wantin' to meet her for almost a year now."

"You mean to tell me she's in your bed, and it's only been a few hours since you met her?"

"Well, yeah. I've been locked up. Remember? And where's your girl? I thought you were seeing her tonight."

"Yes, I saw her, but not the way you see, girls."

"Chadster, Chadster!" Denton put his arm over Chad's shoulder like an older brother about to give worldly advice. "You really are a rookie, aren't you? Didn't they teach you anything in spring training?"

Chad stepped back quickly. "I was there to play ball."

"Man, I'm glad I didn't play winter-ball, and yet, here I am sharing an apartment with a star member of the Fellowship of Christian Athletes."

"Denton, whatever you do is your business, but this is my apartment too, and I don't appreciate you flaunting your womanizing in front of me."

"The bedroom door is closed."

"Where's your sense of decency with women? With your poor attitude, how can you ever expect to have a meaningful relationship that can lead to marriage?"

"Marriage?"

"Yes, marriage! "Did you tell Jasmine that she could park in my space?"

"Well, yeah. You told me that you were gonna see your girl tonight. Let's see, you haven't seen her in over two months, and you're a good-lookin' jock, and she's probably a decent looking chick, so it was only natural for me to assume that you wouldn't be back tonight."

"Well, I am back, and the next time Jasmine comes over…"

"Chadster, Chadster, slow down." Denton's voice was just above a whisper. "You won't have to worry about Jasmine. She's not coming back. It's only for tonight."

Chad lowered his voice to a loud whisper. "Only for tonight! Denton, that's awful. You can't treat people like that."

"Hey, I'm having a good time here, and I'd like to chat a little longer, but I don't want to keep my Jasmine waiting." Denton unscrewed the cap of his beer and tossed it toward the trash can, missing it by a few inches. As he strolled back toward his bedroom, he looked over his shoulder at Chad and said, "We'll talk about this in the morning."

Chad walked to the corner of the living room, away from the bedrooms and reached for his cell phone. He rang up Keith's number.

"Hello." Keith answered as if he were roused from a deep sleep.

"Keith, it's Chad Stevenson."

"It's late, Chad, so this better be important."

"It's very important. It's about Denton."

"Yeah? I was wondering how you were making out with the guy."

"That's what we need to talk about. This guy is like the roommate from Hell. You put me in a situation where I'm forced to be his chauffer, cleaning service, and errand boy. And he's a slob. He drinks all my beer, eats my food, has no consideration for others, and this is only my first day back in Buffalo. Keith, you need to find Denton another place. I'm not going to survive the entire season with that guy."

"Well, don't worry. You won't have to put up with him for much longer. I heard this afternoon that you're being called up to Toronto."

"Really? When?"

"Yeah, really. You're leaving the end of May."

"Man! I can't wait to tell Dad."

"Cool your heels, Chad, and keep this under your hat."

"But this is the best news of my life!" Chad could not contain his exuberance and began to gyrate around the living room in a tribal-like dance.

"You gotta, Chad. I can't go around telling players this sort of news. I could get fired for what I just told you. The front office wants the pleasure of telling you."

"Okay, I won't say a word, but this is so incredible when they haven't even seen me pitch in Buffalo, and now they're thinking of making me a Blue Jay. Wow!"

"They saw enough of you this winter. So, see, you won't have to put up with Denton much longer. Now let me go back to sleep, and we can talk more later."

Chad ended his cell phone call and danced around the apartment. He stopped in the kitchen and opened the refrigerator, where he grabbed the last bottle of beer which Denton had already opened. But all things considered, it was a good day for him.

Chapter 20
Rochester Opener, Then Home to Buffalo

The Bisons had lost their first two season openers, and management was worried that the opposition would sweep their first away-game series. This placed more pressure on Chad who was scheduled to start game three. Eager to see their son's inaugural game, Jane and Arthur dressed up in their warm winter clothes and drove to the Rochester stadium.

The sparse crowd in Rochester, a city perched on the banks of Lake Ontario, reflected the evening's clear and cold April night with temperatures in the upper thirties. As the teams took their traditional places along the baselines for the playing of the national anthem, a blustery wind rushed across the field.

Chad looked around for his parents and was pleased to see them seated in the enclosed VIP section and out of the cold.

"Looks like everyone's bundled up pretty tight in the stands," Chad said to Denton as they stood at attention for the Anthem.

"Yeah. I guess girls won't be shooting us beaver tonight."

"You know what, Denton? You've got a nasty mouth to go along with your mind."

"Chadster, I just can't help it."

"Sure you can, Denton."

In center field just beyond the fence, Denton Fenton noted the well-lit American flag waving so hard he could almost hear it snap in the wind. What's more, it was flying in a direction favorable for a pitcher. He removed his cap along with the other players as the *Star-Spangled Banner* began to play over the PA system.

Denton leaned toward Chad. "Touching music, isn't it? I just love baseball."

Somewhat reluctant to believe in Denton's sincerity, Chad replied with a simple, "Yes."

At the Anthem's conclusion, Chad followed his teammates to the dugout as Denton hustled out to the bullpen.

Though the Bisons had great hitting promise, their prowess wasn't apparent during the first inning, and now it was Chad's turn to take the mound. He pitched his standard warm up routine to the catcher, and the ump called for the first batter. Chad's heart raced slightly with stage fright then calmed as he inhaled a full breath. He was up for the challenge. Rochester might think that they have the better team, but not tonight, Chad thought. *I'm going to give it my very best. These Redwing players are guys from the South, California, and Puerto Rico, but I'm a New Yorker. I'm familiar with this upstate weather. I've pitched this ball in the snow and in the dead of winter since I was five, so this is my game to lose.*

Chad focused all of his energy on the batter and his catcher, shutting out all possible distractions. Unlike his days as a pitcher for the University on Buffalo, baseball was now his career. Even though Minor League ball was only the first rung on the professional ladder, he wanted this to be his finest hour; his moment to show the world that there was always room in any profession for someone with talent.

As the evening wore on, it seemed to be Chad Stevenson's night. Not only had the Red Wings not scored, but when Chad was taken out at the end of the seventh, he had given up no hits and walked no one.

It was time for Denton to close the game with Buffalo's two run advantage over Rochester. By this time in the game, many of the locals would have left the stadium due to the cold weather, except they wanted to see the former Yankee Denton Fenton pitch at their park. Not only that, they wanted to see how he'd pitch wearing a home detention bracelet around his ankle.

"He looks in great form despite wearing that uncomfortable looking ankle device," the announcers said over the PA as Denton warmed up on the mound. "But let's see how he fares against our great Red Wing batters."

Denton watched as the first batter stepped into the batter's box. He carefully positioned himself, went into his windup, and pitched.

"Strike," the umpire called.

"Caught him looking, for a first strike," the announcer added.

The crowd continued to watch as Denton readied himself for his second pitch.

"Strike two, a swing and a miss," the announcer continued. "I tell you folks, this guy Fenton has not lost his touch. That's it, strike three, another swing and a miss, and the first batter is out with only three pitches! That last pitch registered ninety-six on the radar gun. What a great start for Fenton."

To everyone's amazement, Fenton's roll didn't stop there. He put the next two batters out in six more pitches, and while the announcer and the crowd were going wild over the remarkable pitching feat, Denton casually walked back to the dugout.

Chad stood up to meet him while applauding. "Way to go, Denton!" The two struck a high-five. "Now that was impressive."

"Yeah, I was locked and loaded tonight, and of course, I like no-hitters."

"A no-hitter is one thing, but Denton, you just pitched a perfect inning. That's incredible!"

"No sense standing out in the cold any longer than necessary," he shrugged.

"I guess this means you'll want another tattoo on your leg."

"What? What are you talkin' about, Chadster, another tattoo for a simple Minor League performance? I don't think so. Say, where's your girl?"

"I told you. She only plans ongoing to the home games."

"Then have more than one girl. After all, you can't expect the same woman to show up at all your games."

"Melody's my one and only."

"She can't be much in love if she misses your first game as a pro. Sounds to me like she's got another guy."

"I don't think so. Not the way she smiles and looks at me."

"Brother, have you gotta lot to learn. If you wanna keep your girl loyal, then get her pregnant. It'll keep her mind off of other men. Of course, the downside is a screaming rugrat that you'll have to support forever."

"Denton, I just don't like the way you think. Melody is not that kind of girl. She's a sweet lady of sound faith and goodness."

"Then marry her. It sounds like you want to."

Chad paused for a moment. "Well, ya know I just might."

"Too bad because I had a red-head in mind for you, and she plays all positions." Denton's thoughts were interrupted by the sound of a cracking bat. "Would you look at that, Chadster! Aha! Another run. Now your win and my save are well protected. Not bad for your first game as a pro." Denton whistled to the other end of the dugout. "Hey, Keith, I want to ask you something."

Keith walked over to Denton and Chad. He looked at his notes. "It looks like the next three Rochester guys are…."

"That's not really what I wanted. I just want to know what my other teammates think of me."

"What do you mean?" Keith briefly turned around and looked at the other players. "Well, I know they all admire your talent. After all, you were a sensational Yankee, and you just pitched a perfect inning."

"That's not what I mean, Keith. I want to know what they *really* think of me, you know. What do they say about me? What do they call me? I wanna know what these young punks think of this distinguished older pitcher in their midst."

"Well…" Keith's belly had a slight jiggle as he chuckled. "It's sorta funny."

"Sorta?"

"Well, yeah." Keith looked away from Denton.

"Keith! Tell me what they call me. Is it boss, cannon, or Rocket, so what is it?"

Chad leaned in a little closer to hear the quiet conversation.

"Well," Keith hesitated.

"Well, what?" Denton insisted.

"They call you Home Detention Fenton."

"Ha!" Chad blurted. "Now that name has a great ring of distinction."

Denton hung his head low. But his disappointment was short lived when they noticed movement on the field. It was now the bottom of the ninth.

"Guess I'm up." Denton removed his jacket and tossed it on the bench. "Don't worry, Chadster, you're in good hands. I want this save just as much as you want the win."

Denton grabbed his glove and walked out to the mound. He took his time, analyzed his competition, and though it wasn't a perfect nine-pitch side as before, it was three up and three down.

At the umpire's last call, Denton's arms shot into the air like Rocky Balboa, before heading back to the dugout.

"There you go, buddy," Denton said as he shook Chad's hand, "score one for us, and there will be more."

On his way to the showers, Chad thought about his first win. He knew if management had any questions about moving him up, his performance tonight would certainly quell all doubts.

Chapter 21
The Plan to Catch an Assassin

Agent Spence sat down with Marshals Maggie and Bill in the Buffalo conference room to discuss Melody's case. Spence spoke first. "Allow me to report that the thumb drive contained all the necessary reports and research. If the doctor and his wife were still alive, they would be most pleased with Melody for keeping it out of the wrong hands."

"That's encouraging," Maggie said.

Spence continued. "Now, look at this before we start on the subject of Melody and Chad..." Spence placed an article from today's newspaper on the table. "...A local banker was kidnapped and found in a dumpster with his neck broken, a clean murder with no blood or DNA. Does this story sound familiar?"

"Very familiar," Bill said. "It sounds like our professional assassins got a job in our area."

"That's exactly what we're thinking, and thanks to Gladys Cutler, who remembered hearing a name Bose, we were able to narrow him down to this guy." Spence placed a photo on the table. "His name is Bose Bartok, our professional hit man. We showed this photo to Gladys and she confirmed that this was one of the two men."

"Do we know where to find him?" Bill asked.

"Maybe."

"And the other guy?" Maggie asked. "Was Gladys able to get his name? Frankly, I'm baffled why Bose didn't kill Mrs. Cutler, but rather locked her in a closet."

"Apparently, it's not the way these guys operate, broken necks, no guns or knives, and no blood. Besides, after Bose said Gladys reminded him of his mother, she convinced Bose to give her slow death by locking her in the closet. As for the other man, he apparently stayed in the front rooms as a lookout. Gladys never got to see him, but we do have Melody's description of the second guy."

"Do we have any background on Bose? Bill said.

Yes, at nineteen, Bose was signed by the Pittsburgh Pirates but had an early release during spring training. It was his bad attitude and violent temper that did him in."

"What's the plan to find and catch the second perp?" Bill asked.

"We'll use Melody for that," Spence said.

"Now, wait just one minute," Maggie interrupted. "You mean to tell me you would put Melody in further danger just so you can expose and ID the second man?"

"Here's why we know it about Bose Bartok. He seems to always use a second man when carrying out a hit. Perhaps it's the same man that Melody described, sandy hair with a flat-top. Bose will be moving on in a few days, maybe within hours, so every law enforcement agency has his photograph. It's also posted at the border in case he wants to slip into Canada. His dark hair, large jaw, and furry eyebrows are unmistakable. Spreading his photo around has given us a great lead. Bose was spotted in nearby Amherst, and the officer who saw him believes he knows the location of his temporary safehouse."

Maggie chimed in, "I can't imagine the two assassins would travel together or even live in the same place, but surely they communicated in order to plan this latest job on the banker."

"Here's what I'm thinking," Bill said, "and it might be a shot in the dark. We know that Bose Bartok loves baseball, and we have some of the most skilled FBI agents in the field, so if we provide two tickets to the next Buffalo Bisons game, I know the agents can get those tickets into Bose's hands without him even knowing they are from the FBI."

"And then what?" Spence said.

"Melody will be attending that game, and I'll be by her side. To capture both men, we must flood the stadium with undercover cops. All we need is for Melody to make a positive identification of the second man. If she can, then we've got our assassins."

"Or maybe we only get Bose." Maggie added.

"Or neither one, it they don't use the tickets," Bill said. Spence interrupted. "We thought it would be a quiet evening until Melody, called Chad. Our plans obviously needed to be reworked, so here we are. The lookout team placed a tracking device on Chad's vehicle while he was inside Melody's house, so from this point forward, we are able to follow the subject."

"But Melody's protection isn't the only reason we're tailing him," Bill reminded the group. "Chad may be up to his eyebrows in trouble and doesn't have a clue that he is."

Chapter 22
The Vacant Neighborhood

Baseball fever filled the Buffalo air whenever the Bisons played a home game. Fans, sports bars, radio stations, and local television newscasts further fueled the passion, but the only Bison I was interested in was Chad. I just couldn't stop thinking about him. What's worse, I couldn't stop talking about him either. I felt certain that Bill would tire of my constant Chad-talk, but he was a good listener and always polite while I rambled on about Chad. Maybe it was Bill's love for baseball that kept him interested.

"Melody, I'm also anxious to see tonight's game, and know that you'll always have me as an escort to the ballpark"

"Thanks, Bill." He could tell that I was excited to see Chad pitch this evening.

It was early so Bill and I decided to go for a walk. I put on a warm scarf and joined Bill. I hadn't had the opportunity to explore my neighborhood, and now under Bill's watchful eyes, I felt safe to do so.

Bill led the way, and after walking a short distance, he pointed to acres of vacant lots on the other side of the boulevard. "It's safe in this direction."

"Safe?"

"Yeah, there are no neighbors or buildings around to take pot-shots at you."

The large expanse felt, in some ways, like a ghost town where an occasional tree dotted the landscape. As a former Realtor, I found it curious to see continuous cement curbs and gutters lining the streets, punctuated by driveways that led to nowhere.

Bill explained, "Nearly all the houses that once filled these empty lots had been torn down, and only a few remain."

"This looks like a great place to put some spec houses. In fact, why not a whole development? I can visualize a great subdivision here. Perhaps a builder could get as many as a hundred homes in this area. Oh, if only I had the capital, I know exactly the type of product I'd build here." I continued scoping the area. "Golly, I guess I really miss the real estate business."

"Missing it is one thing, but wanting to rebuild Love Canal. Are you nuts?"

"Nuts? What's wrong with my idea?"

"Why, the bad publicity alone is enough to scare away any potential buyers. I suppose you're too young to know about Love Canal?"

"I've never heard of it."

"Back in the seventies, they discovered that over a period of many years an abandoned Hooker Chemical waste site had leeched into the soil that surrounded all the houses in this well-established subdivision. It took a long time for these hazardous toxins to permeate the neighborhood, but eventually the poisons made folks very sick, especially children who were simply playing in their backyards."

I looked down at my feet, then quickly jumped off the grass and onto the sidewalk.

"The residents sued. It was a real mess. Some of the homeowners could see the chemicals oozing through their basement walls, and everyone claimed that the odor was putrid."

"Bill, is it safe to live so close by to Love Canal?"

"At least the Niagara Falls Water Department claims that the drinking water at Love Canal is some of the safest in the city. I don't know about the grounds. That's another matter. Say, Melody, let's grab a bite to eat and head out to the ballpark. Chad is pitching a home game, and neither of us want to miss that."

"Oh, but we'll need to hurry home. I'll need to stop by my house to get our tickets."

While Melody retrieved the tickets, Bill hopped in his car parked in front of Melody's bungalow. Melody joined him. What she didn't see, and neither did Bill, was a man creeping around Melody's back yard and scrounging in her bushes, but as they pulled away from the curb, Melody noticed someone jumping over her backyard fence and into her neighbor's yard.

"Bill, did you see that?"

"See what?"

"Someone was in my backyard. I saw him, just now. A man leaving my yard as he jumped the fence. He's probably in my neighbor's backyard."

"Bill drove the car forward and stopped. "This neighbor's house?"

"Yes, yes, this house! I suspect the guy is still in their backyard?"

"You wait here while I check this out and keep the car doors locked. This is the very thing we need to keep a sharp eye out for. Strangers lurking around your house could put you in danger."

Bill stepped onto the neighbor's front porch and rang the doorbell. A middle-aged woman came to the door.

"Excuse me, ma'am, but my friend, who lives next door, believes she saw a man jumping her fence and into your backyard."

"Good grief!" The woman turned, walked through her kitchen, and yelled out her backdoor. "Monty, come here now."

Monty was a teenager, but with his tall and muscular stature one could easily mistake him for an older man. He entered the kitchen. "Yes, Mom?"

"Monty, were you just now in our neighbor's backyard?"

"Yes, but only to get my baseball. Honest, Mom, I wasn't there more than a couple minutes."

Bill was relived, and returned to the car. A recovered baseball was of no concern, but it demonstrated to Melody the importance of being on guard every moment of the day. "You must believe the companies behind all of this are out there looking for you. They have your photographs and other statistics like your approximate height and weight. You just can't let your guard down for a moment. In fact, I bought you a ladies cloche hat. It's in the glove compartment. Put it on now. The brim will help conceal your face."

"Thank you, Bill, for the hat and for checking on the neighbor. I hope we'll make it to the ballpark before the National Anthem."

Chapter 23
The Setup and the Game

We found our seats a few rows above the first-base dugout. All of Chad's teammates were on the baseline with hats off, standing tall, and waiting for the Anthem when Chad looked over his shoulder and found me in the stands. I had to wave, but Bill snarled with discontent.

"I'm sorry, Bill. I couldn't help myself."

"I realize you're excited to see Chad, but you don't want to get him mixed up in your situation."

"No, I suppose you're right."

"Melody," Bill said sternly under his breath as we stood for the Anthem. "Pay attention to what I'm about to tell you. It's quite important. I want you to look to your left and over my shoulder. There are two empty seats four rows back and in the next section over. See them?"

"Yes, I do."

"When those seats are filled, I want you to see if the men in those seats are the same two who kidnapped and killed the doctor."

"But, Bill, how do you know they'll come to the game?"

"We don't really know, but we managed to give one of the men, whom you could identify, two free tickets to this game. Actually, it was a clever move by one of our FBI agents. They are the best when it comes to this sort of tactic. With any luck, these thugs will show up at this ballgame. We'll need you to verify that both of them are the ones who kidnapped the doctor. So, Melody, now that you know the plan, don't look in that direction until I say, and keep your hat brim turned down. Let me do all the looking."

A few innings later, two men sat down in the seats, carrying beer and hot dogs. Bose's fair-haired partner was with him.

"Melody, I want you to look at those seats and tell me if you recognize the men. Careful, don't pop your head up or move too quickly, but slowly look in that direction, and tell me if you recognize those two men. If you do, turn your head away immediately."

I looked up and recognized both men. My heart raced. I ducked down as if I were picking up something that had fallen by to my feet. "Bill, the man in the tan jacket is the second man."

"Are you sure?"

"Oh, Bill, I want to leave. Those two are the men."

"And we will leave as soon as it's safe."

"Safe?"

Bill called for back-up. "Spence, we have our two assassins here at the ballpark. They're sitting together. You know the seats. Alert your men and stadium security. This could be a victory for us if we can get the needed backup in place. . Without them, this could be a disaster. Send Maggie in and have her meet Melody in the women's restroom near the main entrance."

Melody trembled as she continued to crouch down below her seat.

Bill placed his hand on Melody's shoulder. "I know this is difficult for you, but as soon as I get word that backup is ready, I want you to calmly walk to the ladies' restroom and wait for Maggie. Keep your brim low and don't worry about your long hair. It's your face that I want covered. Maggie won't be long. She's nearby. This place is crawling with officers, and I won't tell you to go until they're in position."

"And then what?"

"Maggie will let you know."

"And what about Chad?"

"I'll take care of him. Just get ready to move. I'll be a safe distance behind you, but once you enter the restroom, I'm going to continue walking out the front gates."

At this time, an announcer's loud voice that blanketed the stadium. "We will now declare the winner of the $100 giveaway sponsored by the Fabulous Pizza and Buffalo Wings restaurant located right here in Buffalo. Everyone, look at your seat number, and now Miss Buffalo will draw and announce the winning seat."

Just then, Bill got a signal that the backup team was almost ready. They asked him for another minute.

"Okay, Melody, stand up and get ready to move."

Remember, Melody, when I say go, walk naturally so you don't draw any attention to yourself. Good luck."

Suddenly, Melody's face was plastered on the stadium's big screen monitor. "We have a winner!" The announcer declared. Please step forward, and our Mascot will escort you down to the field."

Chad pointed to the stadium's big screen and turned to his fellow teammates in the dugout. "That's my girl! She won the door prize!"

At the same time, the two assassins also pointed at the big screen. Bose jumped to his feet and fought his way through the maze of seats, darting toward Melody, while the second guy was immediately handcuffed by nearby agents.

Bill gave Melody a gentle shove. "Go, Melody! Go directly to the restroom and wait for Maggie."

Melody disappeared into the crowd, making it difficult for Bill to stay close.

Suddenly, Melody felt something uncomfortable in her back. Bose pressed something firm against her back and said, "One false move, Melody, and I'll make sure you won't see the next inning. We're going to walk straight ahead and out to the parking lot."

Bill caught up with the Bose and Melody and pressed his gun firmly against the Bose's neck. "U.S. Marshal and, yes, it's my gun that you're feeling."

As Bose turned his head slightly toward Bill, taking his eyes off of Melody, Bill shouted, "Run, Melody! Find Maggie."

Melody dashed toward the ladies' restroom.

Bill forcibly pushed the thug against the wall, which got the attention of Stadium Security who came to Bill's aid. "Mister," Bill said, "as you can see, this place is swarming with FBI and local cops. You're under arrest. See that door on your right that says security? That's where we're going."

Melody made it safely to the restroom, panting hard and trembling. She removed her hat, and dampened a few paper towels to cool her warm face.

Maggie entered the restroom. She looked inside all the stalls and then gave Melody a gentle hug to calm her. "I've asked the front office to have security clear a safe path for us to an awaiting car. The game is suspended temporarily while the agents, local cops, and stadium security remove those two killers from the ballpark. They're announcing a technical issue with the sound system as a cover story so the crowd doesn't panic. We'll wait here until it's safe to leave."

"How will we get out of here?"

"Once we get the *all clear*, which means both men are in custody, we'll walk out of here. Your go-bag is in a waiting car."

"Oh, Maggie! Does this mean I'm moving again?"

"Yes, dear, you're moving again. Melody, are those dark brown roots I see?

Melody stroked her hair. "I'm afraid so."

"Then, once we land in Charleston, South Carolina, we'll get a box of drugstore hair dye and get rid of your blond hair. Changing your appearance will be a very wise thing to do. We need to keep you safe until the trial is over."

"I suppose you're right. Charleston, you say? I like that city."

"We're hoping it will be your last move. The two men being arrested tonight are being charged with murder. At trial, if they wind up with a life sentence or capital punishment, please be satisfied that you played an important role in all of this."

After the two assassins were removed from the ballpark, Bill walked around the outside of the stadium to the ballplayers' entrance, flashing his FBI badge to security. "I need to talk to Chad Stevenson in private."

Inside the locker room, Bill showed his badge to Chad, then the two sat down on the bench. "Chad, you need to understand that Melody is in the U.S Marshal's witness protection program. Tonight, we were fortunate to have arrested the very men whom Melody will testify against in court. Once the trial is over and the men are either imprisoned for life or given a capital punishment, she'll be able to see you as often as you like. However, tonight Melody will be boarding a plane and leaving the state."

"What! She's leaving? Can I see her before she goes?"

"Sure, come with me."

The two walked outside and stood next to the egress road.

"Here she comes, Chad, she's in that car."

As the car neared, Melody rolled down her window. Their eyes locked, and Melody's heart sank.

Chad poked his head in the car and grabbed Melody's hand. He kissed her on the lips, and said, "Will you marry me?"

Melody took in a deep breath and said, "Oh, Chad! Yes, I will."

"Yes! Oh, Melody, I love you so much. I'm a very lucky guy, but they say that you're leaving. Where will you be? How can I find you?"

"Chad, Melody is a very brave woman," Bill said as he pulled Chad back from the car so it could pass. "They have a plane to catch. I'll let you know everything, but first things first. When you return to the mound, win this game for her."

Melody turned in her seat and looked out the rear window until Chad was no longer in view. "Oh, Maggie, did you hear? Chad wants to marry me, and I said, yes!"

The End

More Books from The Author

Dream Season

Shaping Heroes

Jumping Over the Moon

Under the Redbud Tree

Moving Melody

www.ingramcontent.com/pod-product-compliance
Lightning Source LLC
Chambersburg PA
CBHW050738230626
47052CB00003BA/523